KU-130-396

DESOLATION WELLS

After coming to the aid of an oldster, Chet Westoe finds himself being tracked by three unknown riders. A confrontation in the town of Desolation Wells leads to a shootout, but faced with the prospect of jail, Westoe breaks free. He heads for a ranch called the Barbed S, his only clue to the mystery; but there he is entangled in a heap of trouble. The tension builds to a shattering climax as the trail leads straight to an all-out clash with the outlaw gang known as the Bronco Boys . . .

*Books by Colin Bainbridge
in the Linford Western Library:*

PACK RAT
COYOTE FALLS
SHOTGUN MESSENGER
GUNS OF WRATH
SIX-GUN NEMESIS
BLOOD ON THE RANGE
NORTH TO MONTANA
BACK FROM BOOT HILL
TOUGH JUSTICE
GILA MONSTER
HOOFBEATS WEST
FLAME ACROSS THE LAND
BUFFALO WOLF

COLIN BAINBRIDGE

◆

DESOLATION WELLS

Complete and Unabridged

LINFORD
Leicester

First published in Great Britain in 2016 by
Robert Hale
an imprint of The Crowood Press
Wiltshire

First Linford Edition
published 2019
by arrangement with
The Crowood Press
Wiltshire

Copyright © 2016 by Colin Bainbridge
All rights reserved

A catalogue record for this book is available
from the British Library.

ISBN 978–1–4448–4009–4

BROMLEY
PUBLIC
LIBRARIES

AL

CLASS

LPB1F

ACC

03073869

UL

INVOICE DATE

2 1 JAN 2019

Published by
F. A. Thorpe (Publishing)
Anstey, Leicestershire

Set by Words & Graphics Ltd.
Anstey, Leicestershire
Printed and bound in Great Britain by
T. J. International Ltd., Padstow, Cornwall

This book is printed on acid-free paper

1

Chet Westoe came out of the trees riding the buckskin and was close to the summit of the hill when he heard the first shot — it shattered the silence. Immediately he dug in his spurs and galloped to the top of the rise as further shots rang out. Off to his right stood a group of small buildings from which puffs of gun smoke were rising into the air. Westoe reached into his saddlebags and drew out his field glasses. It wasn't hard to pick out the attackers. He could clearly distinguish three of them, skulking from cover to cover. Slipping the field glasses back into their case, he urged the buckskin forwards. The attackers were concentrating their fire on the main building, a cabin from the windows of which issued an answering fire. It was sporadic and he concluded that only one person was in there. The battle was definitely a one-sided affair.

It seemed that the attackers were too intent on pressing home their advantage to notice his arrival. He could see them clearly now. They were all masked and their angles of approach meant that they would soon converge on the cabin. A grim smile lifted the corners of his mouth as he drew his Winchester from its scabbard. At a touch from his spurs the buckskin broke into a gallop, racing down the hill. The thunder of hoof beats finally alerted the masked men to the new danger and they whirled around in consternation. Their guns spewed lead and at the same moment there was a fresh burst of gunfire from a patch of trees further up the hill. Bullets sang through the air as Westoe opened fire with the rifle. One man pitched forward as the other two turned and began to run, twisting and turning as they headed for the trees. Ignoring the danger, Westoe turned his buckskin in the direction of the fleeing men, but they had already reached shelter. He was now in an exposed position and when some scrub oak offered cover of a sort, he took advantage of it. Sliding from the saddle, he crawled forward to where he had a good view of the trees into which the masked men had disappeared. Then he lay flat, raising the rifle and watching closely for any sign of movement.

After a few moments he detected something and immediately squeezed off a shot which was quickly answered by a fusillade of shots that tore up the brush over his head. He rolled over and opened fire again. For a few moments the noise of shooting continued to roar and then there came an unexpected quiet. Westoe lay still, waiting to see what would happen. He was expecting a fresh burst of fire, but instead he presently heard the sound of hoofs and a moment later a group of riders came into view on the far side of the clump of trees, riding hell for leather till they disappeared over a knoll. The sound of hoof beats faded and died and when he was sure they had gone he got to his feet and made his way over to the buckskin. Climbing into leather, he rode back down the hill to the cabin just as the door opened and an elderly man emerged.

'Are you OK?' Westoe shouted.

'Yeah? How about you?'

Westoe became aware for the first time that blood was running down his arm and when he glanced down saw a long cut where a bullet had creased it. Luckily, it was only a flesh wound.

'I'm fine,' he said.

'Those varmints almost got me,' the man said. 'It was sure lucky that you came by when you did.' Westoe dismounted and the oldster noticed his wounded arm.

'That needs seein' to,' he said. 'You'd better come on inside.' Westoe glanced over to where the body of the gunman lay spread-eagled in the grass.

'I'll just check on him,' he said.

He walked across and bent down. The man had been shot in the head and it was immediately clear that he was dead. He turned the body over as the oldster came up behind him.

'That's one less of the varmints,' the oldster said.

'You know who they are?'

'Nope, but they didn't take me completely by surprise.'

Westoe got to his feet and together he and the oldster walked back to the cabin.

When they entered, Westoe glanced around. The place was sparsely furnished. There was a cheap pine table covered with a blue and white chequered oil-cloth and a few straight-backed chairs with cowhide bottoms, some of them held together with baling wire. A wooden box nailed to one of the walls served as a dresser, and on a shelf beneath were ranged a few items such as canned goods, dried beans and coffee. A slab of sowbelly coated with a crust of salt hung suspended from another nail. The windows lacked curtains and a threadbare carpet

5

covered only part of the floor. A few burnished copper pots shone in the fading daylight.

'Take a seat,' the man said.

Westoe did so, taking off his hat and placing it on his knee. The man went to the wooden box and returned with a bottle of iodine and a strip of linen material.

'This might hurt some,' he said.

Westoe flinched slightly as the man poured some of the liquid on the wound and then wrapped it in the linen dressing. 'You struck lucky,' the man said. 'Nothin's broke.'

'I sure appreciate your help,' Westoe replied.

'Not as much as I appreciate yours.' The man paused, thinking for a moment. 'Listen,' he resumed. 'I was just about to rustle up some grub. How are you fixed? I got plenty for two.'

Westoe's first instinct was to move on, but the man seemed to welcome his company. Besides, he was curious about why the cabin had come under attack.

'Sure,' he replied.

'You could put your horse in the corral,' the man said. 'There's feed in the shed.'

Westoe got to his feet and led the buckskin to the corral where he stripped it of its gear and pitched it some hay from the shed. At the outside rear of the cabin there was a washbasin with soap and a towel hanging from a nail. His face and hands were grimy so he washed them both. As he dried himself, he studied the few dilapidated outbuildings and the country at the back of the cabin before returning indoors. He couldn't help noticing that the place had a run-down kind of look about it.

For a moment he was surprised to find the room empty, till the oldster appeared in a doorway carrying two bowls and two spoons.

'Hope you can put away some stew,' he said. 'I had it simmerin'.'

He placed the bowls on the table and they both sat down. Westoe took a spoonful of the stew; it was hot and almost burned his mouth, but it tasted good. He took another before speaking.

'You said somethin' about not bein' completely taken by surprise. Do you know who these varmints are that attacked you?'

The man thought for a moment and then replied with another question. 'You're not from around these parts?' he said. Westoe shook his head.

'Just passin' through,' he replied.

'On your way to anywhere in particular?'

'Nope. I just figured it was time to look for new country.'

The man got to his feet and went back through the door from which he had emerged with the stew. When he came back he was carrying two big tin mugs of coffee which he placed next to their bowls on the table.

'Then you won't know anythin' about the trouble that's been happenin' round here,' he said, as if the conversation had not been interrupted.

'What kind of trouble?'

'It's kinda hard to pin it down. Just trouble. Cattle rustlin', stagecoaches bein' robbed, people gettin' shot. There ain't any regular kind of pattern. I figure it's just a bunch of no-goods cuttin' loose. I never figured they'd try pickin' on me, though. I just don't see any sense to it.'

'What'll you do? They might come back.'

'I can take care of myself. They don't bother me.' Westoe was thinking that the outcome might have been a lot different if he hadn't come by when he did.

'You run this place all by yourself?' he asked.

'Yeah. I guess I should be thinkin' of movin' on, 'specially now the old lady is gone, but I just can't seem to want to make the effort. I guess me and her spent too long together here.'

Westoe guessed, from the state of the cabin, that the oldster had been alone for some considerable time despite the impression his words gave of his wife's demise being a recent event. But he didn't pursue the matter.

Westoe finished his bowl of stew and wiped his mouth with the back of his hand. He took a sip of the coffee, then reached for his tobacco pouch and took out the makings before handing it to the oldster. When they had lit their cigarettes the man grinned.

'Guess we'd best introduce ourselves. I'm Ben Howe.'

'Chet Westoe.'

They sat back, enjoying the taste of the tobacco, and occasionally breaking the silence with a comment. Westoe glanced at his companion from time to time. It was clear that he appreciated the company. Despite the oldster's profession of unconcern, he felt worried on his behalf. He thought of the dead man outside. There was a good chance that the gunnies who had attacked the old man would come back, seeking revenge. He felt reluctant just to leave him.

'Listen,' he said at last. 'You and me had better do somethin' about buryin' that *hombre* outside. After that, maybe I could stick around for the night, just in case the others or even more of 'em decide to come back again.'

'That's mighty decent of you to offer, but didn't you say you were passin' through?'

'I'm not in any hurry. It's up to you. I could bed down in the barn.'

'No need to do that. I can make a mattress for you right here on the floor.'

Westoe could sense a feeling of relief in the man's words. 'OK,' he said, 'then it's settled. You got a shovel? Then let's get on and do what needs to be done.'

Burying the gunman took longer than they had anticipated and by the time they had finished night had fallen.

'I'll go make up that mattress,' the oldster said.

'Good,' Westoe replied. 'While you're doin' that, I'll just check on my horse.'

He made his way back to the corral. At his approach the buckskin came up to the fence and he stroked its mane. All around, the country lay still and bathed in moonlight. Any sounds would travel and he felt confident that he would wake if there was any suggestion of danger. He had considered staying awake and keeping watch, but he felt tired. Besides, he didn't want to alarm the oldster unduly. It was unlikely that anything would happen, but he would keep his gun loaded and close to hand. With a few whispered words to the horse he made his way back to the cabin.

As he had expected, nothing happened during the night. He didn't get much sleep, however, because of the old man's snores. At the same time, his arm gave him some discomfort. He was kept awake, too, by his own troubled thoughts. He felt a certain hesitation about leaving the oldster, but he was reluctant to stay. The spread was clearly in a rundown condition and Howe didn't seem to have anybody to help with the running of the place.

As the first rays of dawn began to lighten the gloom, Westoe finally threw aside his blanket. He walked to the door, opened it and peered outside. The eastern sky was pale and the last stars were fading. He felt some compunction about leaving the oldster, so he decided to stay on for the rest of the day and help the old man sort out some of his more urgent problems as regards the upkeep of the ranch. That would allow the immediate danger from the men who had attacked the ranch to pass. After that, the oldster would have to take his chances. In the meantime, there was work to be done about the place.

The day passed quickly. Howe seemed glad of his help, and he tipped in with surprising energy. They started by carrying out a few repairs about the cabin and the outbuildings and cleaning out the shed which passed as a stables. The corral needed attention and when they had done that they rode further afield to check the state of the fences.

Some of them were slack and they hammered in fresh staples. As they rode, Westoe acquainted himself with the lie of the land. The ranch was small and the cattle he saw looked under-nourished. When they got back to the cabin late that afternoon and were enjoying some strong black coffee, he asked to see the tally book. The oldster looked at him with a hang-dog expression.

'I can't remember what I did with it,' he said. 'There are some papers in a drawer in the kitchen.'

Westoe went to have a look. There was a whole pile of old papers and documents scattered about but no trace of a tally book.

'How much stock do you reckon to have?' Westoe asked the oldster.

'I ain't sure. Around five hundred head I reckon. Me and one or two of the other small ranches kinda join forces at roundup time.'

'Well, I reckon you could do with takin' stock before that time arrives.' He

14

finished the coffee and got to his feet.

'I guess you've got to be on your way,' the oldster said. Westoe wasn't sure whether it was a statement or a question, and for some reason he found himself avoiding the man's eyes.

'What about that arm?'

Westoe held it out and flexed the muscles. 'It'll be fine. I sure appreciate everythin' you've done for me.'

'It's me should be thankin' you,' the oldster replied. 'If you're ever back this way — '

'I'll be sure to look you up,' Westoe interjected. 'In the meantime, maybe you should think about hirin' somebody.'

The man nodded, but didn't say anything as Westoe walked to the door. He went outside and made his way to the corral, the oldster following close behind. He stood in silence while Westoe saddled up and fastened the girths tight. When he had finished, Westoe turned to him.

'I don't figure you'll have more

trouble from those varmints,' he said. 'I reckon we did enough to scare 'em off.'

'Yeah. Like I said, they don't worry me. They're more likely to pick on somebody else than come back here.'

Westoe swung himself into the saddle. 'Thanks again,' he said. 'Be seein' you.'

He touched his spurs to the buckskin's flanks and rode out of the corral. He didn't want to drag things out. Only when he had covered a little distance did he turn to see the old man standing there, still watching his departure. Despite himself, he felt a strange pang. Was it guilt? But what did he have to feel guilty about? Was it pity? He knew the ravages that emotion could bring; it was one to be avoided. The oldster was probably right when he said he could look after himself. He wasn't responsible for everybody who crossed his path. He had done his bit to help. He suddenly felt a return of the feeling he had had earlier that day and he felt a surge of gladness that he was back on the trail again, looking forward to making his camp with a breeze stirring in the trees, the howl of a coyote for company and the stars wheeling overhead for a roof.

★ ★ ★

Holden Stroup, the owner of the Barbed S ranch, sat his horse and looked down on the wide sweep of rangeland spread out beneath him where cattle were grazing in profusion. It would soon be time for the roundup and then the trail drive to the railhead where he expected to make a good profit. He breathed in the soft air fragrant with the sweet smell of grass. The sky was clear and blue, with away in the distance a smudge of white cloud over the hills. He almost felt the weight of the sun as it fell on his shoulders. He squinted his eyes, peering into the distance, and watched a rider he had just spotted heading in his direction. The man was riding fast and approaching them rapidly. For some reason, he felt a sudden chill go through him and he turned to his foreman who was next to him.

'Do you recognize that man, Barnet?' he asked. The foreman looked closely.

'I'm not sure, but it looks like someone who used to work here until fairly recently. O'Neil, I think they called him.'

'He sure seems to be in a hurry.'

'He's coming from the direction of the ranch house,' Barnet remarked inconsequentially. They stopped talking as the man got closer, only slowing as his horse climbed the slope of the hill. Finally he stopped close by and took his hat from his head by way of acknowledgement, but seemed reluctant to speak.

'Well,' Stroup said after a few moments, 'what is it? I assume it's me you're in such a hurry to see.'

The man seemed to fumble about, seeking the right words. 'They told me you were over this way,' he said. 'I got over just as quick as I could.'

'If you've got somethin' to say to Mr Stroup,' Barnet snapped, 'you'd best get right on and say it.' The man crushed the brim of his Stetson between the thumb and forefinger of his right hand.

'I'm sorry, Mr Stroup,' he said. 'I'm afraid I've got some bad news.' Stroup's face had blanched.

'It's about Eben, isn't it?' he said. The man nodded.

'He's been shot.'

'Shot?'

'There wasn't anything we could do. We were taken by surprise. It was a plain case of bushwhackin'.'

'Never mind that,' Stroup snapped. 'Where is he now? He'll need a doc.' The man shuffled uneasily in the saddle.

'I'm afraid it's too late for that,' he said. 'Eben's dead.' Stroup seemed to rock visibly in the saddle.

'Who did it?' he mumbled.

'It was a stranger. We were just passin' by old Ben Howe's place when

19

we came under fire. I don't know. Maybe the old man thought we were trespassin' or somethin'.'

'What? You mean Ben Howe killed him?'

'Not exactly. We had just taken cover when this stranger came by. It was him did it.'

'Where is Eben now?'

'Still there. We had to leave him.'

'Then how do you know he's dead?' The rider looked blank as the dazed look on Stroup's face suddenly became one of anger.

'When did this happen? Today?'

'Nope. It was the day before yesterday.'

'And you've taken till now to tell me?'

Stroup looked as though he was about to strike the man who glanced guiltily at Barnet as if he expected to find some kind of protection from that quarter. Stroup struggled for a moment to get his anger under control.

'I've got a pretty good idea what you

were doin' out at the Howe spread,' he finally snapped. He turned to his foreman. 'Go on back to the ranch and roust up a few of the hands. Then join me.'

'Where will you be?'

'At the Howe spread, of course.' He turned back to O'Neil. 'You come with me,' he rapped.

Without waiting for a reply, he dug in his spurs and sped away, quickly followed by O'Neil. The foreman took a few moments to watch them before addressing some remarks to his horse.

'Well,' he drawled, 'I guess this don't come as any surprise. The only pity is it wasn't his brother. If anybody deserved to get shot, it was Rafe. Mr Stroup sure didn't deserve any of this.' He gathered a ball of spit in his mouth and spat it out in a high arc.

'Come on, feller,' he said. 'Let's do as Mr Stroup says.'

2

Westoe drew his buckskin mare to a halt beneath a tree from which hung a weather-worn board on which were carved the words: *Desolation Wells*. It hung at a crazy angle so it was impossible to tell which direction it indicated. After a few moments spent in contemplation, he got down and inspected the ground. His practised eye detected traces of three horsemen having passed that way. A faint smile passed across his countenance. He was aware they had been following him for at least the previous two days, but he had eluded them and now they had gone on ahead. There was little doubt that if he continued to follow their sign, he would catch up with them in town. It was an old trick, but it seemed they had fallen for it. He had simply ridden down into a stream-bed and followed its course for a couple of miles before doubling back on himself. Who they were, he couldn't imagine, but he would soon find out. He could have challenged them at the stream, but he had thought better of it. He had no desire to get involved in a shooting match, and he had a better chance of avoiding one if he confronted them in town. So right now they were the pursued and he was the pursuer.

As he rode, he continued to think about who they could be, but he couldn't come up with any answers. Dusk was falling and only the creak of leather and the occasional snorting of his horse relieved the silence. His eyes peered into the distance and eventually he detected a glimmer of light and the first vague outlines of buildings. There were trees lining a narrow stream which curved at a sharp angle and he clattered across a narrow plank bridge over the dark, murmuring water. The street beyond was deserted, but after continuing a little further he came to a junction and turned into what was obviously the main street of the town. There were people about and some of the stores were open. He was looking for a saloon and it didn't take long for him to see one. There were horses tethered outside. Coming to a halt, he slid from the saddle and tied his own mount to the hitching rail before pausing to take a look at the other horses. Three of them bore the same brand: *The Barbed S*. The name meant nothing to him, but he had no doubt they were the horses the men who had been following him had been riding. He paused for a few moments, still thinking, before stepping up on to the boardwalk and shouldering his way through the batwings.

Inside, the saloon was dense with smoke, but it took only a moment for him to see two of the three men who had been following him standing at the bar with their backs to him. He looked around for the third one, but he had only viewed them through his field glasses and didn't recognize anyone who might answer the part. He moved forward past groups of people sitting at tables or playing faro and blackjack. There was a piano in a corner, but the pianist had vacated his stool. Some saloon girls circulated among the crowd and one of them approached him, but he brushed her aside. He reached the bar, put his foot on the rail and observed the two men through the ornate mirror behind the counter. One of them looked vaguely familiar, but it could have been anyone he had met. The other one he didn't recognize, but the type was unmistakable. They wore their guns slung low. He glanced at the barman who was standing at the end of the counter talking to a customer; after a final word he came over.

'Whiskey,' Westoe said.

The barman poured and Westoe took a sip. He looked in the mirror again and saw one of the men staring at him. If he recognized him, he wasn't letting it show.

'You boys headin' some place in

particular?' Westoe said. The man exchanged glances with his companion.

'What's that to you?' he said

'Nothin', except you've been followin' me for the last couple of days.'

'I don't know what you're talkin' about.'

'Those horses standin' outside with the *Barbed S* brand — I take it they're yours?'

The man looked awkward. He wasn't sure how to react or what to say. As he stood trying to work out what to do, Westoe observed his companion edge away from the bar. He had been hoping to avoid trouble, but it looked like it was coming his way.

'You're not denyin' you've been on my trail?' Westoe said. The man's expression darkened and the puzzled look became one of anger.

'I don't know what you're game is,' he said, 'but if you're accusin' me of somethin' you'd better take it right back.'

'I'm accusin' you of followin' my

trail,' Westoe replied, 'and I want to know why.'

There was a moment's silence. Some of the other people in the saloon had caught on that something was happening at the bar and turned their faces in that direction. One or two towards the centre of the room were surreptitiously shuffling their chairs further back and the batwings suddenly creaked as a few of the customers at the rear of the room made their exits. Suddenly the man's hand moved towards his holster, but Westoe was too quick and, as the six-gun appeared in the man's hand, Westoe's .44 spat lead. The man reeled sideways, catching his companion as he fired in turn so that the shot whistled harmlessly over Westoe's shoulder and thudded high up the saloon wall. Steadying himself for just a moment, Westoe fired two more shots and then ducked to one knee before firing again. The noise of gunfire was deafening. People were shouting and screaming and he heard the glass of the mirror shatter as gun smoke filled the air. Bullets were ricocheting round the room and a chandelier hit the floor with a loud crash. When the shooting stopped and he had a chance to take stock, Westoe saw the two men both lying stretched full length on the floor. He rose to his feet and walked over to where they lay, taking care in case they were only feigning or wounded. It only took a moment, however, for him to ascertain that they were both dead. He looked up at the bar-tender whose ashen features had just appeared above the counter.

'You saw what happened,' he said. 'I acted in self-defence.'

The barman nodded as the silence of the room was broken by a few concurring voices and then a hum of excited comment and conversation. From somewhere behind the bar the swamper appeared with a bucket and broom.

'Somebody had better get the under-taker,' Westoe said.

Just at that moment the batwings flew open and the sheriff burst in, his revolver in his hand. Westoe looked him over. He looked to be in his early forties, lean and in good condition. He came forward and examined Westoe with clear, steely grey eyes.

'You responsible for this?' he snapped.

'They started it,' Westoe replied. 'All these folk can witness to that. I was only defending myself.' The sheriff looked around before trying the barman.

'Is it true what he says, Lorne?' he said. The barman nodded.

'I don't know what started it off, but those two were the first to draw.'

The sheriff paused for a moment before sliding his six-gun back in its holster and turning to Westoe.

'I think you and me got some talkin' to do,' he said, 'over at the jailhouse.'

Westoe was about to remonstrate, but something about the sheriff's demeanour suggested it might be better to comply. 'Sure,' he said. 'I ain't got nothin' to blame myself for.'

With the sheriff right behind him, he passed down the saloon and out through the batwings. He continued walking in the direction of the jailhouse. When they had reached it, the sheriff indicated a doorway leading to his office and stepped inside. Somewhat to Westoe's surprise, the sheriff invited him to take a chair before reaching into a drawer from which he produced a bottle of whiskey which was about half full, and a pair of tumblers.

'Guess we could both use this,' the sheriff said, pouring. Westoe took the proffered drink and threw it down his throat. The sheriff's eyes were looking closely at him. Westoe held out his glass and the sheriff refilled it.

'I'm Sheriff Snelgrove,' he said, 'and I like to keep a tight ship, so I guess you'd better do a good job of persuadin' me why I shouldn't throw you behind bars right now.'

'I don't know what this is all about,'

Westoe said, after introducing himself in turn. 'What I do know is that three men have been following me for the last couple of days — maybe before. I let them get ahead of me. I could have fixed them back on the trail but I was kinda curious about what they were up to. I let them get ahead of me. They made for this place.'

'Desolation Wells — it's better than it sounds.'

'I figure I'll reserve judgement on that for the time bein'.'

The sheriff took a swig of his whiskey before leaning back in his chair. 'I checked on those horses outside the saloon too,' he said. Westoe looked up quickly. 'Oh yes, I keep my eyes open to everythin' that goes on around here,' Snelgrove continued. 'So what do you know about the *Barbed S*?'

'Nothin' at all. Except those three riders seem to be connected with it.'

'And what about a man named Stroup, Eben Stroup?' Westoe's brows puckered as he considered the question.

31

'Nope,' he said after a few moments' deliberation, 'can't say as I've ever heard the name.'

The sheriff gave him a quizzical look. 'Now that's kinda strange,' he replied, 'considerin' that I've been told you're responsible for murderin' him.'

'You mean . . . '

'Yeah. I had a word with one of them. I figured I needed to know what they were doin' in town. I'd be more likely to get the truth from one than if I asked them all together.'

'Look, I don't know what's goin' on. I've never heard of anyone called Stroup.'

Snelgrove finished his whiskey and placed the glass carefully on the table. 'Hell,' he said, 'I don't even know why I had to get involved in this, but since I'm the representative of the law round these parts, I guess I'd better do somethin' about the situation. I ain't sayin' I believe either him or you, but it's clear someone's lyin'.'

'That's easy settled,' Westoe said.

'Bring that varmint who told you I'd killed this Stroup feller over here and we'll see who's tellin' the truth.' The sheriff grinned.

'You might have a point there,' he said. He stretched and yawned. 'One thing I always figured, however, is that a man tends to think a whole lot better when it's daylight than he does in the dark. This little matter can wait at least till morning. In the meantime, I can offer you the comforts of a cell for the night. You'll be needin' someplace to stay and I'll make it as comfortable as I can and even throw in some grub into the bargain. You must be feelin' kinda tired after all this activity.'

'What about the other man? The one I guess you were talkin' to.'

'Don't you go worryin' about him. He won't be goin anywhere till I say so. Mind, I don't like to think what his reaction will be when he hears how you dealt with his two companions.'

'What else did he tell you?'

'Nothin' much. In fact, strangely

33

enough, he more or less confirmed what you just told me. Leastways, that they'd followed you almost as far as Desolation Wells and you were likely to be hittin' town soon.' The sheriff yawned. 'It's gettin' late,' he said. 'What do you think to my offer?'

'About a cell for the night? Seems like I ain't got any choice.' Snelgrove nodded.

'That's the way to look at it,' he said. He glanced across to the wall on which hung a bunch of keys. Westoe was thinking rapidly. He couldn't make head or tail of what he had got himself into. The sheriff seemed like a decent sort, but a night spent in jail didn't appeal to him. One night might somehow get stretched to another and then more. Who could tell what the *Barbed S* rider might allege against him? Stuck behind bars, he wouldn't be able to do anything to help himself. As Snelgrove began to rise from his chair, he had made up his mind.

For only a moment Snelgrove's back

was towards him, but it was long enough. In an instant he leaped to his feet and kicked the desk over, sending the sheriff tumbling to the floor. Before Snelgrove had time to recover, he was through the outer door of the office and dashing across the street to where his horse was tethered. Without any hesitation he swiftly untied it, vaulted into the saddle and wheeled away, galloping hell for leather down the street. He glanced behind him and saw Snelgrove just emerging from his office. He thought he heard a shout and then a bullet whistled over his head. He ducked and lay low across the buckskin's back. Another shot rang out but he was almost out of range and in a few more moments he had reached the junction and was out of sight. His horse was fast and he had a head start of any pursuers. He let the mare have its head and was soon clear of the town and lost in the darkness of the night. He kept riding, intending to put a lot of distance between himself and Desolation Wells

before sunup. He didn't really anticipate any pursuit, at least not till the
morning. Whether Snelgrove would be
concerned to get up a posse at that time
seemed unlikely, but he couldn't rule it
out. He had committed no crime, apart
from the minor assault on the sheriff.
As he settled the horse to a steady jog,
he thought about what had happened.

He couldn't make it out. What were
the facts? Three men, apparently from a
ranch called the *Barbed S*, had been
trailing him. One of them had accused
him of murder. They must have got the
wrong man. Well, it was really none of
his business. He was tempted just to
carry on riding and shake the dust of
the region from his feet. But would he
ever be free of suspicion till the matter
was properly resolved? What was the
name of the murdered man? The sheriff
had mentioned it. He racked his brain.
Eben Stroup, that was it. Quite an easy
name to remember. If he had ever come
across someone with that name in the
past, he would have recalled it. So the

whole affair must be a matter of mistaken identity.

Shortly before dawn, satisfied that he was safe from pursuit, he drew the buckskin to a halt in the shade of some trees and dismounted. Quickly, he built a fire and placed a slab of bacon in the skillet. He made coffee with water from a nearby spring and settled down to enjoy breakfast. While he was doing so, he relaxed and he stopped thinking. When he had eaten he got out his packet of Bull Durham and rolled himself a cigarette. Somewhere nearby an oriole began to call. The first tints of light appeared in the sky. These were the times he enjoyed. Despite not having slept for almost twenty-four hours, he felt alert. As he began to think back to the night's events, he had a feeling that the sheriff's shots had been meant more as a vain attempt to bring him to a halt rather than anything else. He recalled the shouting which had only just reached his ears. Whatever Snelgrove thought of the whole affair, he didn't have enough against him to want to shoot him. After all, it was only his word against that of the three men from the *Barbed S*. What was it all about? Suddenly he knew what he had to do. There was only one final way to clear his name. He would find out the truth of the Eben Stroup affair. The only real clue he had was the *Barbed S* connection. His first step was to find out just where the *Barbed S* was located and make his way there. He could pose as a ranch-hand looking for work. It would soon be roundup season and there was every chance he would be taken on. From that point on, he would just have to play it by ear and trust his intuition.

There were only two things to worry about. If a murder had taken place and someone at the *Barbed S* suspected him of it, would he be recognized or mistaken for the real murderer? The *Barbed S* meant nothing to him, but he couldn't be sure he wouldn't be riding into a hornet's nest. The second thing was a bigger concern. What would happen if and when the remaining rider returned to that ranch? If he decided to carry on the pursuit, he might be delayed, but sooner or later he would be back. There was no time for delay. He would need to act quickly. And from the moment he set foot on the *Barbed S* range, he would be on borrowed time.

With some reluctance, he finished his cigarette and set about removing all traces of his campsite. When he had finished, he threw his saddle over the mare, tightened the girths and climbed into leather. He had no idea where the *Barbed S* ranch was, but he figured that if he retraced his steps to the point at which he had first become aware of the three riders following him, he would be in a better position to find out. It must lie somewhere near there. With a glance towards the sky, he turned the buckskin in that direction.

★   ★   ★

After watching Westoe disappear, Sheriff Snelgrove's first reaction was to saddle up his mount and ride after him. A few moments' reflection were enough, however, for him to see the futility of giving pursuit. Westoe had a good start. He had no idea which way he would decide to go and it would be impossible to find his sign in the darkness. His pride had been wounded, but it didn't make any sense to go off at half-cock. A few people emerged on hearing the shooting, but he waved them away and went back inside to pour himself another drink. When he had restored his equanimity he got to his feet, took a bunch of keys from a drawer, and locked the outer office. He returned and went through a doorway which led to his own private apartment. Without removing any of his clothes, he threw himself down on his mattress and lay awake looking at the ceiling.

He was up early next morning, having slept but fitfully, and after a quick breakfast, made his way through to the office. He looked out of the window. The place was beginning to stir and presently he saw the remaining *Barbed S* man making his way over. He opened the door and the man entered.

'I'm sorry for what happened last night, Barnet,' he said. 'It is Barnet, isn't it?'

The man muttered a surly assent. 'I warned you about that *hombre*. Couldn't you have done somethin' to stop him shootin' my friend?'

'Friend? There were two of 'em.'

'Yeah. One was a regular rider for the *Barbed S*. In fact, it was me took him on in the first place. Mr Stroup assigned the two of us to the case. I don't know how the other feller got involved. To tell you the truth, I don't feel any regrets about him bein' killed. I never took to him.'

'The way I heard it, it was your friends who started the whole rumpus. You can count yourself lucky you weren't there.'

The man sat down in a chair beside the sheriff's desk. 'The question now is, what do you intend doing about it?' he said.

The sheriff observed him as he sat beside him, straddling the seat. Despite his protestations, he didn't have the air of someone in mourning. After a significant pause it was the sheriff who spoke.

'Tell me again about Westoe,' he said, without preamble.

'Who?'

'The man you were following. The man who shot your friends.'

'I told you already,' the man replied.

'Tell me again.' The man glanced sideways at the sheriff.

'Well, like I told you before, we've been on his trail for a couple of days.'

'Because he killed Eben Stroup,' Snelgrove interrupted. 'Remind me; who exactly is Eben Stroup?'

'He's one of Mr Stroup's sons. Mr Stroup is the owner of the Barbed S.'

'One of his sons?'

'There's another one called Rafe.'

'And what makes you think this man Westoe shot Eben?'

The man shifted uncomfortably. 'Because there was a witness. He told Mr Stroup about what happened.'

'A witness? A reliable one?'

'I don't know,' the man exclaimed. 'I guess you'd have to ask Mr Stroup that question. I'm only followin' instructions.'

'What would Westoe have against him?

'Like I say, I'm just followin' orders. I'm not the one you should be askin'. All I know is that Mr Stroup set us the task of trackin' him, actin' on information received.'

Snelgrove looked closely at Barnet. He couldn't tell whether he was telling the truth or not. Instead of pursuing that line of questioning, he took another.

'With what purpose exactly?' he asked.

'Look,' the man blustered, 'we coulda dealt with Westoe our own way, but Mr Stroup ain't that kind of a man. He wants Westoe to face justice.'

'After what happened last night, it sure don't look that way.' Snelgrove stroked his chin. 'You've put me in an awkward position,' he continued. 'This whole affair ain't really any of my business, but as the representative of the law round these parts I can't just let it go.' He paused, thinking hard. Eventually he looked up.

'I'll say one thing,' he resumed. 'I don't figure Westoe is guilty.'

Barnet looked at him sharply. 'How would you know?' he said. 'Where is Westoe now? Haven't you put him under arrest?'

'Let's just say he left in a kind of hurry. But that don't mean I want you to go doin' anythin' hasty.'

'If you can't do anythin' then I sure am,' the man snapped.

'Now what did you just say about wantin' to keep things legal? OK, listen up. Can you be ready to ride in half an hour? I'll meet you right outside the saloon.'

'What? You're formin' a posse?'

'Just the two of us. We'll see if we can find Westoe. But I ain't got a lot of time to spend on this. If we can't find him fairly pronto, you're on your own. I got plenty of other things I need to do without goin' off on a wild goose chase. Like I say, I'm willin' to give it a try, but if Westoe's lit clean out, then that's it.'

Without waiting to argue the matter, Snelgrove rose to his feet. The *Barbed S* man looked less than happy as the sheriff ushered him out of the door. Snelgrove watched his retreating figure till it was lost to view and then took in a deep draught of the morning air. He had made a compromise with the *Barbed S* man and with himself. He didn't see what else he could do. Personally, he didn't hold out much hope of finding Westoe, but at least he would have done something.

* * *

After a day and a half, the country through which Westoe was riding began to change and presently he discerned a range of low-lying hills dotted with clumps of trees. As he got nearer, he spotted a wisp of smoke in the distance. He rode towards it and presently saw a ramshackle structure in the lee of a boulder-strewn slope. It was part tent and part cabin and as he got closer he could read the words *Bowman's Store and Trading Post* scrawled in faded letters. A couple of horses were standing at a hitchrack in the yard.

'Well,' he said, addressing the buckskin, 'seems like we might be in luck, old girl.'

So far he had come across no-one and he had been wondering where he might get the information he needed regarding the whereabouts of the *Barbed S*. Maybe someone at the trading post would be able to supply information.

He rode up, dismounted and tied his horse next to the others. He could hear voices coming through the open doorway and one of them seemed to be that of a woman. Taking the time to look around him, he listened to the voices for a few moments, but couldn't make out what they were saying, and then he stepped through the doorframe. The air inside was warm. Two men were standing at the counter, behind which stood a tall woman with a pretty face and her hair tied back in a bun. A kettle hissed on top of a potbellied stove. The woman broke off her conversation with the two men and glanced up at his arrival. For a moment their eyes met and they held each others' gaze, then she said in a lilting voice:

'I'm makin' coffee. Would you like some?'

'That would be right welcome, ma'am,' Westoe replied.

She nodded towards a table and he sat down at it. In a few moments she had poured the boiling water and brought him a piping cup of strong black coffee. As he took his first sip, he glanced at his surroundings. Although the room served as a store, there had been some effort to make more of it. In addition to the table at which he sat, a few chairs were placed near the stove. The empty windows were covered in rose-patterned chintz and there was a threadbare carpet on the uneven floor. Flowers stood in pots and vases on whatever surface provided a space, most of which was piled high with supplies and sundry items such as metal bowls, wooden boxes, picks and shovels. A trestle laid across a couple of barrels formed a rude counter.

'Is there gold in the hills?' Westoe asked, addressing the two men who were looking at him surreptitiously.

'Used to be,' one of them remarked. 'It's just about cleaned out by now.'

The woman was regarding him with her face tilted a little to one side. 'Are you aimin' to pan for some gold?' she asked.

Westoe looked at her. The way she asked the question suggested something teasing in her manner.

'No ma'am,' he said, 'I'm just passin' through.'

'Then you'll maybe be needin' some supplies?' she said.

'Sure, I could use a few things.'

'Which way are you headed?' one of the men asked.

Westoe saw his chance to raise the issue which was on his mind. 'I'm lookin' for a spread called the *Barbed S*,' he said.

His reply seemed to act like a cold douche. There was a pause. One of the men produced a pouch of tobacco and a corncob pipe which he proceeded to fill. He tamped the tobacco down but instead of lighting it, put it back in a pocket of his jacket.

Before Westoe had finished his coffee, the woman came across and took his cup away.

'Maybe you know of it?' he resumed. 'If so, I'd sure appreciate you tellin' me the way.' His words hung heavy in the changed atmosphere. He was feeling awkward and not sure how to continue when the woman spoke.

'Take the trail at the back of the store and just keep on ridin'. It's still quite a long ways. When you pass some old diggin's you'll come to a wide valley runnin' east and west. Follow it to the end.'

'I'm much obliged,' Westoe replied. He got to his feet and began to pick out some items he would need for the ride ahead. Although nothing more was said, he was conscious of three pairs of eyes on his back. He returned to the counter, carrying the articles he had selected.

'Maybe I've got this wrong,' he said, 'but I get a definite impression that I've said somethin' to upset you folk.'

'Nobody's upset,' the woman replied.

'Look. If there's somethin' about this *Barbed S* ranch you ain't tellin' me — well, I'd appreciate if you just out and said what it is.' The woman handed him his supplies in a bag without replying and he laid his money on the counter.

'You got business with the *Barbed S*?' the man with the corncob pipe enquired.

'Only lookin' for a job. I got experience of range work. I figure they might need someone now it's getting along towards roundup time.'

'There are other ranches,' the man replied.

Westoe couldn't think of a ready answer to that one so after a moment's hesitation he took the bag and made for the door. He stepped out into the sunlight and strode over to the buckskin. As he was adjusting his saddle bags to accommodate his purchases, he heard a light footstep behind him and turned to face the woman.

'Maybe we were a mite unfriendly back there,' she said. 'It's just that some of us got cause to have some suspicions about the *Barbed S*.'

'Suspicions?' he prompted. She hesitated as if uncertain to say anything further, and he was touched to see that she bit her lip.

'I don't want to prejudice you,' she said. 'Go on and if you get a job at the *Barbed S*, then see for yourself. There's no proof of anythin'.'

He looked closely at her. Lines were spreading on her face and her hair was beginning to grey; he figured she must be around forty years old, but she still held her looks and charm. Before he could say anything else or ask any further questions, she turned away and went back into the store. For a few moments he wavered, adjusting the girths, then he climbed back into the saddle. Touching the horse's flanks with his spurs, he rode round the cabin and set his course for the hills.

Just ahead of him, near a clump of trees, was a boulder off to the side of the trail. He would have passed it by, but there seemed to be some writing scrawled across it. Veering towards it, he dismounted and took a close look at the rude lettering. It read:

Sean Bowman. Born 1834. Died 1873.
A Loving Son. Secure In Your Hands.

Westoe drew his hand across his chin. Sean Bowman? The lady's son? Whoever it was, his death was recent. He thought of the woman's last cryptic words: *'There's no proof of anythin'.'* What did she mean by that? Was it a reference to this man's death? For a moment he felt an impulse to go back and question her further, but it quickly passed. It was none of his business to go probing another person's wounds and sorrows. There were many unanswered questions he could have asked, but he had learned enough to set him on his guard in matters relating to the *Barbed S*. Climbing back into leather, he continued along his way.

3

Shortly after the conclusion of their conversation, Marshal Snelgrove and Barnet rode out of Desolation Wells, heading west. It seemed logical to assume that Westoe would carry on riding in the same direction he had been before arriving in town. They rode slowly at first, looking for sign. There were various traces of horses which might have been left by Westoe's buckskin, but there was no way of knowing. All they could do was to carry on riding and hope to pick up something more positive. They continued till mid-morning when Snelgrove called a halt to give the horses a break. As they rested in the shade of some trees, Snelgrove pulled out his pouch of Bull Durham and, after taking some tobacco and papers himself, handed it to Barnet. When they had rolled cigarettes and lit up, he turned to the *Barbed S* man.

'Tell me again, what's your connection with the *Barbed S?*'

'I'm foreman. Been there quite a while.'

'The *Barbed S*,' Snelgrove repeated. 'Is it a big spread?'

'Near three thousand head of longhorn steers,' Barnet replied.

'And it's owned by a man named Stroup?' Barnet nodded. 'Just tell me again. What was the name of his other son; I mean the one who didn't get shot?'

The man glanced away and when he replied there was a look of distaste on his features. 'Rafe,' he replied.

'I get the impression you're not too fond of him,' Snelgrove said.

'I don't have any opinion.' Barnet paused for a moment as if a thought had suddenly occurred to him. 'Hey, wonder if that other feller Westoe shot was one of Rafe's friends? That would account for him stringin' along.'

'The one you said you didn't take to?'

'Yeah.'

The sheriff paused, looking around him. 'Gettin' along to roundup time pretty soon,' he eventually remarked. Barnet nodded.

'We need to find Westoe and bring him in quick now,' he replied.

Snelgrove glanced back along the trail they had been riding. 'I wouldn't count on catchin' up with him,' he said. There was no reply and they drew on their cigarettes.

'What'll you do if we don't find him?' Snelgrove asked.

Barnet paused indecisively. 'That's somethin' I'm just gonna have to think about,' he commented.

Snelgrove took a last drag of his cigarette and then flicked the stump away. 'You can think about it while we ride,' he said. 'We ain't gonna do our chances of catchin' up with Westoe any favours by sittin' around here.' He got to his feet and Barnet followed suit.

They quickly remounted.

'Hell, this is hopeless,' Barnet remarked. 'We might be goin' completely in the wrong direction.' Snelgrove eyed him closely.

'You're right,' he replied. 'I'm gonna give this till nightfall and then I'm callin' it a day. After that you're on your own. Do what you think best, but there's one thing I gotta say.'

'Yeah? What's that?' Barnet asked.

'Whatever you decide to do, I'd prefer not to see you around Desolation Wells again.'

★   ★   ★

After leaving the trading post, Chet Westoe had hoped to reach the *Barbed S* that same night, but it gradually became clear that the ranch was further than he had thought. Accordingly, towards midnight, he decided to set up camp by a stream sheltered by a grove of bushes. After picketing the buckskin on a grassy patch close to the water, he gathered sticks and soon had a fire started. When he had eaten and drunk a couple of mugs of strong black coffee, as the fire died down he lay back with his head on his saddle and his shoulders covered with the saddle blanket. For a long while he lay awake, thoughts darting through his brain, till eventually he nodded off into a fitful slumber.

He was awakened by the cold. He stirred the ashes and added some more twigs and leaves. He didn't feel much like eating and made do with another brew of coffee. Then he saddled up the buckskin. The sun was still below the horizon when he rode out. He was worried in case he had missed the abandoned diggings mentioned by the woman at the trading post, but as the light began to spread he realized he must have entered the wide valley she had mentioned. At least it was a similar one. In the growing light, he could see that the hillsides were dotted with aspen and ponderosa pine. As he rode on, he began to notice signs of riders having passed that way and eventually he saw ahead of him cattle standing singly or in small groups. It was obvious that he was on range land and he soon caught his first glimpse of the ranch. The main ranch house was a two-storied building behind which stood various outbuildings and a corral with a number of horses in it. Westoe sat the buckskin for a few moments, taking in the scene. The ranch looked prosperous and well suited to its surroundings. After a time the door to what Westoe assumed was the bunk house flew open and two men came out. They made their way to the yard where a couple of horses were tied to a hitchrack, mounted up and rode slowly away. Westoe watched them till they disappeared behind a rise, then touched his spurs to the buckskin's flanks and rode down to the ranch house. He dismounted and then stood for a few moments considering his next move. He hadn't given much thought as to what he would do when he arrived at the *Barbed S*. He had simply been intent on getting there. Now that he had found the place, he was still in a quandary. He was saved from further thought when a man appeared around the corner of the ranch house and approached him.

'I saw you ride up,' he said. 'Is there somethin' I can do for you?'

'I don't know. I was hopin' to have a word with the owner.'

'Mr Stroup? He's overseein' somethin' down on the north range.'

'The owner of this spread is called Stroup?' Westoe asked, for confirmation.

'Sure. I guess that's why they call it the *Barbed S*. S for Stroup, I mean.'

Westoe nodded. 'Yes, I see.' He stopped, observing the quizzical look on the other's face.

'Is it a job you're lookin' for?' he asked, after a moment's pause. 'If so, you might just be in luck.'

'As a matter of fact, that's what I was hopin'.'

'Then you could have a word with Jack Sumter. He's actin' in the capacity of foreman while Mr Barnet, the regular foreman, is away on business. He ain't here just at the moment either.' There was an awkward pause and then the man resumed: 'Tell you what. Come on over to the bunk house. I'll roust up a cup of coffee and you can wait till Mr Sumter gets back. He shouldn't be long.'

'Sure sounds like a good idea to me,' Westoe replied.

The young man grinned. 'My name's Lucas,' the other man said, 'Lucas Bunch.'

'Chet Westoe. Glad to make your acquaintance.'

They shook hands and were just about to make their way to the bunk house when they heard a clattering of hoofs. They looked up as a rider galloped up and swung from the saddle. He regarded the two of them for a moment before speaking.

'Who the hell is this?' he snapped.

Westoe was observing the way his companion appeared to withdraw into himself as the rider addressed him. He seemed to be steeling himself to reply when Westoe answered for himself.

'The name's Chet Westoe,' he said. 'I was just introducing myself to this young man.'

'Well, now that you've done that, you can get back on your horse and ride right out again.'

Westoe took a moment to observe the new arrival. He looked to be in his late twenties, narrow-built, with deep-set eyes and hollow cheeks. Something about him made his scalp crawl. Bunch seemed to be winding himself up to speak.

'Mr Westoe was just askin' whether there might be a job for him. I said he would have to speak to Mr Sumter.'

The newcomer turned his gaze on Bunch. 'Well,' he said, 'he doesn't need to stick around and talk to Sumter now. I've just told him he can leave.'

'I didn't intend to cause any kind of

trouble,' Westoe interposed. 'If you say you don't need any extra hands, then that's fine by me.'

'Good,' the man snapped. He turned again to Bunch. 'Take my horse and give it a good feed and rub-down.' With a last fierce glance in Westoe's direction, he turned on his heel and marched into the ranch house.

'Sorry about that,' Bunch said as the door swung shut.

'He sure don't seem too happy. Who is he?' Westoe asked.

'That's Rafe Stroup.' Westoe's attention quickened at the name.

'Rafe Stroup?' he repeated.

'Yeah. He's Mr Stroup's son.'

'The only one? How many sons does Mr Stroup have?' As soon as he had spoken, Westoe realized that his words were somewhat hasty. He glanced at Bunch but couldn't detect any reaction. The young man seemed not to see anything suspicious about the question.

'There were two of 'em; Rafe and Eben. Now there's only Rafe. Seems like Eben got himself killed, but I don't know the details because nobody seems to want to talk about it.'

'When did this happen?'

'Just recently.

'Well,' Westoe replied, attempting to cover up his previous indiscretion by seeming disinterested, 'I guess it's none of my business.' He moved to the buckskin and climbed into leather.

'I'm sorry about the coffee,' Bunch said, 'but I guess I'd better do what Mr Stroup says.'

'Sure, thanks for the offer.'

'If you really need that job, I guess you could try again when Mr Sumter is back.' Westoe nodded.

'I might just do that,' he said.

'Rafe probably won't be around for long. He tends to come and go. We don't see that much of him.'

'Then I guess I just called at the wrong time,' Westoe said. 'Thanks again. I'll see you around.'

Without more ado, he turned the buckskin and rode out of the yard. As

Bunch watched him, the door of the ranch house flew open again and Rafe Stroup emerged.

'I thought I told you to attend to that horse!' he snapped.

'Just doin' it,' Bunch replied.

He turned to the roan gelding which Rafe had just been riding. It was sweating and had obviously been driven hard. As he untied it, he was relieved to see Rafe walk away in the direction of the bunk house. He led the horse to the stables and was just removing the saddle when the door opened and three men swept in. Ignoring him, they saddled up their horses and led them out; through the open door he saw them mount and gallop away. He remained motionless for a few moments, deep in thought, before turning his attention back to the job in hand.

Westoe had no intention of giving up on the plan of getting himself a job at the *Barbed S*. If what Bunch had told him was correct, he had simply chosen a bad moment to arrive at the ranch. He would give it a day or so and then try again. Maybe he would have better luck with the older Stroup or with the temporary foreman, Sumter. He had learned quite a lot already from Bunch. If the regular foreman was away, could he be one of the three riders who had been following him? His plan now was to set up camp somewhere in the hills and return to the *Barbed S* in due course. In the meantime, it would be no bad thing to get to know something of the lie of the land.

After traversing a relatively flat area of ground, the trail began to wind up over some further hills with patches of wooded land through which he rode slowly, savouring the pungent smell of the trees. Sunlight dappled the path and the sound of the breeze whispering in the leaves was a pleasant accompaniment to the creak of leather. Then suddenly he thought he detected another sound, a faint muffled thud. Maybe it was nothing, but his instincts told him to be careful. Swiftly, he slid from the saddle and pushed forward though the trees on foot. Then he stopped, listening and waiting. The sound reached his ears again, the tread of hoofs on soft earth. He drew his six-gun and waited till he saw a vague hint of movement through the trees. He pressed himself close against the trunk of a pine and watched closely as two riders came into view, one of them riding a distinctive skewbald. They drew to a halt, looking about them and then down at the ground. It was clear to Westoe that they were looking for the buckskin's tracks. After a moment one of them looked up and then immediately went for his gun.

Westoe realized he had been seen and loosed off a couple of shots. The man jerked backwards and then toppled from the saddle, his gun exploding as he did so and sending a bullet crashing into the branches high overhead. Immediately the other man dropped from his horse and took shelter. Westoe was just about to move around the side of the tree behind which he was hiding when he heard scraping noises behind him and turned to face the new danger, but he was too late. He felt a blow in his back like a hammer had been swung and the roar of a shot close by. He fell forward, rolling over as another shot thudded into the bark of the tree just over his head. A fog began to descend as he crawled away and then he felt himself falling into a dark abyss of pain and unconsciousness.

When he came round again, it was dark and the trees arching overhead looked like sinister sentinels watching over his corpse. For what seemed a long time he lay inert, not feeling anything till pain began to gather and grow in his shoulder. At least it confirmed to him that he was not dead. Setting his teeth against the pain, he managed to raise himself to a sitting position so that he could look around. It seemed he had fallen into some sort of gully, the sides of which were quite steep. He lay among a tangle of bushes and other vegetation which had presumably broken his fall and hidden him from the sight of anyone looking down from above. His head throbbed and he had to make an effort not to lose consciousness. When he tried to move, pain shot through him and he knew he was badly hurt. He needed to think. Were his assailants still around? He listened for any sounds of movement but could hear nothing, save the whisper of the wind in the trees. Then he realized it was no longer daylight. How long had he been lying there? The sky above his head was just beginning to grow light so he guessed it was approaching dawn. The attackers, whoever they were, had obviously left him for dead. He needed to get out of the gully and find his horse. Would it still be there? And if it was, would he have the strength even to haul himself into the saddle? There was only one way to find out.

Bracing himself for the effort, he

struggled to his knees and then, wincing with pain, managed to stand upright. His back felt sore and tender all along its length and he guessed that the bushwhacker's bullet had raked it. His left shoulder was bloody, but as far as he could tell, nothing was broken. Suddenly he remembered his gun. He looked about and to his surprise saw it lying among the vegetation. He reached down and retrieved it, wiping it free of mud and leaves. Then, placing it in its holster, he took in some deep draughts of air and started to climb. Ordinarily, it wouldn't have been difficult, but in his condition each step was an effort. He grasped at whatever hand and foot holds he could find and slowly began to ascend. His eyes had grown accustomed to the dark and he could see well enough as he inched his way forwards through the brush. Towards halfway he began to feel an almost irresistible temptation to stop and rest, but he knew he couldn't take the chance of losing consciousness again. He had to keep going. Suddenly his feet slipped from under him and he slid a little way backwards, gasping with pain, till a vine brought him to a halt. He lay still, gathering his strength, and then began again.

The climb seemed interminable, but at last he hauled himself over the rim of the gully. Grey light was filtering through the trees and the first thing he saw was the buckskin. The sight gave him fresh energy and, drawing himself erect, he began to hobble towards it. As he did so he felt blood flowing down his back where movement had caused his wound to open up. A shaft of light coming down though the foliage threw the horse into relief; he was getting closer to it when he suddenly stopped. The buckskin was tied to a tree. It was a trap. Not being sure whether they had finished him off or not, his attackers had left at least one man behind to kill him if he should reappear. Even as the thought struck him he saw a stab of flame and a bullet whined close by.

71

Stopping suddenly in his tracks had probably saved him. In an instant he had taken cover and drawn his own revolver. Another shot thudded into the tree behind which he had taken cover, sending shards and splinters of bark raining into the air. He had a good notion of where the attacker was hiding, but was he alone? Another shot rang out, coming from the same direction, and he was convinced that there was only one man. He waited for the next shot. The buckskin was a little way further down the track and he had a sudden fear that the gunman might shoot it or it might be hit accidentally. Still he waited. His back ached and stung and his head felt heavy and as if a clamp had been fastened to the back of his skull. Minutes passed, but there was no further shooting. His ears strained for any faint sound that might indicate that the gunman was trying to outflank him, but he could hear nothing. He was worried in case he might pass out. Maybe the time had come for him to take the initiative.

He hunkered down and was about to move when his ears caught the unmistakable sound of boots scuffing the earth. He took the chance of peering round the tree and saw a glimpse of a fleeing figure hurtling through the trees. Instinctively he made a move to follow, but he was pulled up by the pain in his back. Even disregarding his injury, he was too exhausted to mount a pursuit. He was only relieved that the man, whoever he was, appeared to have had enough. Having missed his first shot and the opportunity to finish off his victim at no risk to himself, he had decided to take no further chances. Westoe holstered his gun and then staggered onwards, but before he had reached the buckskin he heard the sound of hoofs through the trees. The man had made good his getaway.

It seemed to take a long time to reach the tethered horse. His knees were shaking and he felt woozy. His eyes seemed to be out of focus and he feared he was about to faint. As he came up to it, the buckskin shied and then stood still as he untied it. For a few moments he stood beside it, summoning his remaining strength to make the supreme effort of climbing into the saddle. He gripped its mane and placed one foot in the stirrup. His arms and legs felt weak and watery and it seemed he wouldn't be able to throw his other leg over the horse. Gritting his teeth, he put out all his energy and succeeded in getting astride and spurring it into movement. He swayed in the saddle and then lay low over the buckskin's back. He knew he was badly hurt and he needed to find help, but he had no idea in which direction to go. Too weak to care, he let the horse take him where it would. After a time the trees thinned and they emerged into more open country. Light was flooding along the eastern horizon, heralding another day.

★　★　★

It was in the early hours of the morning that Sheriff Snelgrove returned to Desolation Wells. True to his word, he had continued the search for Chet Westoe till the evening before deciding to abandon the enterprise. He had known from the start that it was a hopeless quest, but he had felt it was his duty to make an effort. The way Westoe had escaped still rankled, however. Barnet had seen it as just another indication of Westoe's guilt, but Snelgrove was less than convinced. Despite his best advice, Barnet had decided to carry on the search.

'Even if you catch up with him, what will you do?' Snelgrove asked. Barnet shrugged.

'I liked Eben,' he said. 'He had his faults, but he wasn't a bad boy. More than that, I owe it to his old man. Me and Holden Stroup go back a long ways. We rode together before he struck it rich and acquired the *Barbed S*.'

'I wish you luck,' Snelgrove said.

One thing puzzled the sheriff slightly. Barnet seemed a decent sort. If the accounts of what had occurred at the saloon were to be believed, that was more than could be said for his two companions. According to the eyewitnesses, it was they who had started the trouble and been the first to draw iron. It didn't seem to fit. Barnet had certainly expressed his dislike for one of them. Maybe he was wrong about Barnet. Maybe he would have acted just like the others if he had been there at the time.

The streets of the town were black, but as he rode down the main drag and approached the jailhouse, he was surprised to see a lamp still burning in his office. He would normally have taken a backstreet in order to reach the lean-to stable at the back of the building, but instead rode up to the front and tied his horse to the hitching rail. He stepped up on the boardwalk and turned the door-handle to his office. It opened and inside he found his deputy sitting and smoking a cigarette.

'Howdy Drabble,' he said. 'I didn't expect to find you here at this time of night.' He sat down in a chair and put his legs up on the table. 'Well that was a waste of time,' he continued. 'I can think of a heap of things I'd rather have done.'

'You didn't catch up with your man then?' Drabble said.

'Nope. Didn't really expect to neither. Anyway, you haven't explained why you're up so late. I hope nothin's wrong.'

The deputy took a last drag of his cigarette before stubbing it out in an ashtray. 'No,' he said. 'Things are quiet. But there's somethin' I figured you'd like to know. The undertaker was over this afternoon looking for you. He seemed quite excited.'

'Then it must have been somethin' important. It takes a lot to get Henry Wilkins interested.'

'Seems so. He said for you to look

him up tomorrow. In the meantime, he left a message. Seems like one of the men that feller Westoe shot was none other than Dwayne Oliver.' The sheriff started and put his feet back on the ground.

'Dwayne Oliver! Is he sure about this?'

'Sure as he can be, unless there's more than one *hombre* got a jingle-bob ear and a death's head tattooed on his back.'

'Dwayne Oliver. Well I'll be.'

Drabble looked across at Snelgrove. 'Is it true what they say about him?'

'Every last word of it. Dwayne Oliver is one of the meanest gunslingers this side of hell.'

'If that dead man is Dwayne Oliver,' Drabble mused, 'then Westoe must be one heck of a fast gun.'

'Oliver has a reputation for bein' a back shootin' snake,' Snelgrove responded.

His expression was thoughtful. 'I guess this kinda throws a whole new light on this little affair,' he said. 'Those three men claimed to have come from a ranch called the *Barbed S*. Now what would someone like Oliver be doin' ridin' for it? I tell you what. It sure makes me more convinced than I was before that Westoe is an innocent party.' Again he asked himself the question: what was Barnet doing riding with Dwayne Oliver? And if what Barnet had said about Oliver being a friend of Rafe Stroup was true, what did that say about Rafe?

'I don't know exactly where that *Barbed S* spread is located,' he said, 'but it seems to me that if varmints like Dwayne Oliver are nestin' there it spells a heap of trouble for Snake County.' The deputy glanced up.

'You figure if there's somethin' goin' on at the *Barbed S*, that it might spill over?' The sheriff's face was grim.

'Not if I have anythin' to do with it,' he said.

Drabble rose to his feet. 'Guess I'd better try and get some shuteye,' he remarked. Snelgrove walked him to the door.

'Thanks for waitin' up,' he said.

'That's OK. I couldn't get to sleep anyway. See you in the mornin'.' The sheriff glanced up at the sky.

'That won't be long,' he replied. He watched his deputy as he walked away down the empty street before going back inside. He sat down and put his feet back up on the table. When it was daylight he would get straight over to the undertaker. In the meantime, there was no question of his turning in for the rest of the night. He had too much to think about.

★   ★   ★

A jolting movement caused Chet Westoe to open his eyes. The sun was shining out of a clear sky. His back hurt with the swaying movement and he realized he was being carried somewhere. One pair of arms supported his shoulders and another held his legs.

Then the sunlight was suddenly cut off as they entered a building. He turned his head and though he couldn't see much of it, the place looked vaguely familiar. There was a distinctive aroma which he thought he recognized but couldn't place. He was carried through a doorway and then laid on a mattress, face down. His head sank into a pillow. There were voices:

'Take care removin' his shirt.'

'Hell, it's kinda stuck to him. He's gonna start bleedin'.'

'Be as gentle as you can. That wound needs attention.'

One of the voices was a woman's and he struggled to remember where he had heard it before. Then he recalled whose voice it was and knew where he was. He made a move to sit up, but a strong hand pushed him gently back.

'Mr Westoe, isn't it,' the woman's voice said. 'I'm Leonae Bowman. You're at the trading post. You stopped by here once before.'

'I don't understand . . . '

'The horse brought you in. You were unconscious. I don't know how you didn't just fall out of that saddle. Now, don't ask any more questions. You've got a bad wound that needs dressin'. I'm afraid it's going to hurt.'

She stopped talking and he could hear some stirring around. Then he felt hands tugging at his shirt. Waves of pain shot through him, but he gritted his teeth. He was sufficiently aware to know the woman was right. He needed help if he was to pull through. He felt something probing his wound and then he passed out again.

When he came round, he was immediately aware of pain, but it was less than it had been. He wasn't able to sit up straight because the wound had been dressed and he was swathed in bandages. He turned his head to take in his surroundings. The room was plain, but pleasantly furnished. The sun streamed in through a window and on the ledges were vases of flowers. A sampler hung on the wall bearing an image of a church with a tall spire and some hills in the background. He noted the name in one corner: *Leonae Bowman*. He turned his head the other way and was surprised to find that he was not alone. Somebody was sitting in a cane-bottomed chair at the head of the bed. Westoe looked up as the person moved the chair closer and then couldn't help but let out a muffled gasp of surprise.

'Ben Howe,' he muttered. 'What in tarnation are you doing here?' The oldster's face creased in a grin, revealing a few jagged teeth stained with brown.

'I was about to ask you the same question,' he replied. Westoe shuffled about and managed to drag himself more upright.

'Be careful,' Howe said. 'You don't want to go bustin' that wound open again after everythin' Leonae's done to fix it up.'

'What am I doin' here?' Westoe said. 'I don't remember much after gettin' on board that buckskin.'

'I don't know how she found her way here, but you owe that old hoss. I was sittin' right outside when I saw her comin'. I could see there was somebody slumped across her back, but I never figured it'd be you.'

'I got bushwhacked,' Westoe said.

'Then maybe it was the same bunch of no-good hombres burnt down my cabin and drove me out.'

'What? Those varmints came back after all?'

The oldster was thoughtful. 'I guess it must have been. It's funny though. If it was them, they didn't return at once. Before they arrived, I had a visit from someone else — Holden Stroup. He's the owner of a big spread called the *Barbed S*.'

Westoe made to sit up, but only succeeded in causing himself pain. 'Holden Stroup? I know the name. In fact I'd just paid a visit to the *Barbed S* when those coyotes dry-gulched me. What did he want?'

'That man you shot — it turned out he was one of his sons.'

Westoe was trying to concentrate on the oldster's words even though his head was beginning to pound. 'So that's why they burnt you out?'

'I don't figure it that way. Mr Stroup had reason to be angry, but he wasn't. He just wanted to know what had happened. I told him straight and he seemed to understand. I can tell you I was mighty nervous, but he didn't seem to hold no grudge.'

'What did he do? Just go away?'

'He went away all right, but he took the body with him.'

'Took the body?'

'Got a couple of his men to dig it up right there and then. I can't say I had any regrets about seein' it go.'

'Let me get this straight,' Westoe said. 'Holden Stroup came after I left and took away the body of his son. And he didn't try to exact any revenge?'

'Nope. Like I say, he was good about it.'

'So when did your cabin get burned down?'

'That came later.'

'How much later?'

'A couple of days. A bunch of riders came. Luckily I saw 'em comin' and made my getaway. I would have faced up to them, but they were just too many.'

'I should have stayed. Sorry. I didn't figure somethin' like that would happen.'

'It weren't your fault. I ain't the first it's happened to either. I might have cut and run this time, but I intend goin' right on back and buildin' me another cabin and if there's a next time, I'll be sure to be ready for 'em.'

Westoe's head was full of thoughts and he was just about to ask the oldster some more questions when the door opened and Leonae appeared carrying a tray.

'Don't let Ben tire you out now,' she said. 'Here, I've brought you some broth. You need to regain your strength.'

With the help of the oldster, she gently helped to raise him a little bit higher so his head rested on the cushion. She placed the tray beside him.

'Do you think you can manage by yourself?' she asked.

Westoe nodded and, dipping a spoon into the broth, lifted it to his mouth and swallowed it. 'That sure tastes good,' he said.

'How does your back feel?'

'Not so bad, considerin',' Westoe replied.

'It should be OK. I've cleaned and dressed it a couple of times. It doesn't seem to have got infected.'

'I don't know what to say,' Westoe replied. 'I've got so much to thank you for.' She looked at him quizzically.

'Did you make it to the *Barbed S*?' she asked.

'Yeah. I had the pleasure of meetin' Mr Stroup's son. He wasn't exactly friendly.' Leonae and the oldster exchanged glances.

'It was not long after that I got shot,' Westoe said. 'There were at least three of them. I accounted for one. I only escaped because I fell down some kind of ravine. One of 'em waited for me, but my luck held. He rode off when his plan went wrong. A pity. I'd have liked to take a look at his horse.'

'His horse?'

'To check the brand. I don't know what reason they would have for wantin' to kill me, but I got a hunch those bushwhackin' varmints were from the *Barbed S*. Seems kinda funny otherwise.' He had finished the broth and Leonae took his tray.

'We can talk later,' she said. 'Come on, Ben; let the man get some rest.'

With a nod in Westoe's direction, the oldster followed her out of the room. Westoe would have liked to ask a few more questions, but Leonae was right. Even the effort of sitting up and drinking the broth had left him feeling weak and exhausted. Nevertheless, he felt that what Howe had said was important. His head hurt and he felt slightly dizzy and confused. What was it the oldster had told him? He felt he was on to something. He lay back and drifted into an uneasy sleep.

4

Darkness hung over the *Barbed S* like a drawn curtain. Clouds scudded across the sky and through the blown patches of space a few faint stars gleamed. Only one light cast a muted glow through an open window in the study where Holden Stroup sat up late. In his hand he held a glass of brandy which remained untouched. After a time he put it down and, getting to his feet, walked across the room to a wall of shelves which held his library of books. He glanced along one shelf and took a book in his hands before gently putting it back again. He moved to the window and listened to the sounds of the night; the soughing of the wind, the snicker of a horse in the corral. Although it was dark, he thought he could discern the little mound and the new gravestone which marked the resting place of his son. He suddenly felt a profound sense of loss. Why did it have to come to this? He had heard the story of what had happened at the old man's cabin from Howe himself and he had no reason to doubt the truth of his words. He wasn't stupid. He knew the sort of company Eben had got involved with. Not only that; he knew who had influenced Eben to stray — his brother Rafe. Reluctant to accept the truth, he had tried to make excuses for Rafe, but there were some things he couldn't deny. For example, that it was Rafe who had led Eben on. But then, he had to accept responsibility as well. He was Rafe's father. If Rafe had turned out badly, then ultimately it was his fault. If their mother hadn't died when they were young, it might have been different. That was no excuse, however. Throughout their childhood and youth he had failed to give Eben and Rafe the time and attention they needed. He had been too occupied with building up the *Barbed S* when his priority should have been tending to their upbringing.

He turned back inside the room and sat down again. He picked up the untouched glass of brandy and took a swig, rapidly followed by another. The warmth of the liquid felt good and helped to restore him a little. Maybe it wasn't too late. Maybe not everything was lost. There was still time to get through to Rafe. After all, the ranch would fall to him now that Eben was gone. Perhaps he could be brought to a sense of his responsibilities. He couldn't have gone too far along the route to dissolution. Sure, he had heard some talk about Rafe's activities, but he refused to believe the rumours. He would make a point of having a good talk with Rafe in the morning. He had been hard at work on the range and hadn't seen or heard anything of him, but Bunch had assured him that Rafe had returned to the ranch the previous afternoon. Surely, too, Rafe was affected by the death of his brother. Something like that couldn't fail to have an impact. He would discuss everything with Rafe and have it out with him, really clear the air. Things would be different. Somehow, some good would come out of Eben's death. He emptied his glass and poured another. By the time he had drunk that he felt ready to retire. Getting to his feet, he closed the window and then turned down the lamp before leaving the room, closing the door gently behind him.

* * *

Lucas Bunch could vouch for the fact that Rafe Stroup had returned to the ranch earlier the previous day, but he did not see him ride out again the following afternoon. While his father was reflecting on events and planning to talk to him the next day, Rafe had left the *Barbed S* far behind. He rode hard, heading deep into the range of hills and camping overnight, till late in the morning he approached a narrow defile. When he had almost reached it he brought the horse to a halt and, raising his head, gave vent to a version of the old Rebel yell. The echoes of it were still reverberating round the hillside when it was answered by another yell and the figure of a man armed with a rifle appeared from behind some boulders near the top of the hill. He peered down at the lone horseman.

'Is that you, boss!' he shouted.

'You've got eyes in your head. Of course it is.'

The man didn't respond as Rafe spurred his horse and rode forward. Initially the passage barely allowed for more than one horse and rider, but it opened out to reveal a high tight valley circled by hills. Lying in the shelter of a hillside stood a number of rude huts, cabins and corrals. Bunches of rustled cattle stood idly cropping the grass. It was a perfect outlaw roost. As he rode down, a couple of figures emerged from the largest cabin and stood awaiting his arrival. He drew up and slid from the saddle and one of them, taking the reins, led the horse away.

'I could do with a drink,' Rafe snapped.

He strode through the open door of the cabin, followed by the other man, and flung himself down on a settee. The man moved to a cabinet from which he took a bottle of whiskey and a glass. He poured a stiff drink and handed it to Rafe.

'Have one yourself, Skinner,' Rafe said. The man did so and then seated himself in a straight-backed chair opposite Rafe.

'We didn't expect to see you back so soon,' he ventured to say.

'No point in hangin' around.'

'How is your old man?' Rafe shot Skinner a hostile glance, but seemed to relax quickly.

'He's OK.'

'You told him about burnin' out that oldster's cabin?'

'Nope. In any case, that was for my

satisfaction, not his.'

'I just thought . . . '

'Don't think anythin'. You're not here to think. None of you are here to think. You're here to do what I tell you.'

'Sure, boss.'

'How are the boys?'

'It was fun settin' fire to that oldster's place, but they're already gettin' kinda restless.' Rafe was silent for a moment.

'That's good,' he continued, 'because I've got somethin' in mind, and this time it ain't cattle rustlin' or burnin' down shacks. I don't know about you, but I'm gettin' kinda tired with all that small-time stuff. I figure it's about time we really put the name of the Bronco Boys on the map.' The other man took a big swallow.

'The Bronco Boys?' he said.

'Yeah. That's us. The way I figure it, we need a name for folks to remember us by. We need to instil some fear, some respect into 'em.'

Skinner took another sip of the whiskey. Then he turned to Rafe with

96

an ugly grin twisting his thin slash of a mouth.

'The Bronco Boys,' he repeated. 'I like it.'

Rafe gave a sudden laugh. 'Listen,' he said, 'I been thinkin' and I got a lot of plans.'

'Yeah? Like what?'

'Like holdin' up the bank at Desolation Wells for a start.'

'Desolation Wells. Ain't that a bit out of our way?'

'That's exactly what I've been sayin'. We need to think big. We need to extend our range if we don't want to stay a bunch of nonentities. I don't know about you, but I'm ready to make a name for myself that will be known all over the West. Are you with me?'

Skinner finished the last of his glass. He sat silently for a few moments and then let out an unexpected whoop.

'Hell and damnation,' he almost shouted, 'do you need to ask? Of course I am.'

Any lingering trace of animosity

between them seemed to have vanished as Rafe leaped to his feet and poured another couple of drinks. When he had done so he turned to Skinner and raised his glass.

'Then here's to the Bronco Boys,' he said. 'So far, we ain't done nothin', but just as soon as Dwayne gets back, all hell is gonna break loose!' He paused for a moment. 'Why even wait for Oliver? We've got the explosives. We don't need nothin' else.'

They both broke into a prolonged series of whoops and yells before finishing their drinks and then emptying the bottle. When they had done so, Rafe got to his feet and headed for the door.

'Where are you goin'?' Skinner said. Rafe turned his head.

'I figure the boys ought to know what plans we got in store, don't you?'

'The Bronco Boys, you mean.'

They burst into raucous laughter once more as they staggered out into the sunlight.

* ★ ★

Sheriff Snelgrove had other things to do apart from worrying about the little matter of the Dwayne Oliver shooting, but one afternoon he dug out from the recesses of a cabinet a sheaf of Wanted posters and among them he found the one he was looking for. Dwayne Oliver was accused of carrying out a string of shootings in several States and there was a substantial reward for anyone bringing him in dead or alive. He folded the poster and put it in his pocket. Again, he began to wonder what a gunslinger like Oliver would be doing in the vicinity of Desolation Wells. Even more to the point, what was his connection with the *Barbed S*?

He was pursuing these thought when he was roused by a distant rumble which he thought at first was thunder, but quickly realized was the sound of galloping hoofs. The sound diminished and then came again, increasing in volume. His instincts told him that there was danger and, dropping the poster, he turned quickly to a rack of guns hanging on the wall and took down his old trusty 1866 Model Winchester. He jammed shells into it from a cabinet and then ran out into the street. The sound of approaching horsemen was getting louder and one or two people walking by turned their heads and looked questioningly into the distance. At the same moment his deputy ran up, carrying his own rifle.

'I don't like the sound of it,' Snelgrove snapped. 'Quick, follow me.'

He began to run towards the sound of the hoof beats and carried on running till he and Drabble had cleared the central part of town. The thunder of hoofs drummed in their ears and out of a cloud of dust they saw a group of riders coming on fast.

'Take cover!' Snelgrove rapped. Drabble hesitated.

'What about you?' he said.

'Don't worry about me. If they . . . '

He didn't get to the end of the

sentence as a gun suddenly barked, followed by others. Snelgrove and the deputy both ran for shelter in the shadow of the nearest building as a cacophony of noise tore their eardrums and lead flew willy-nilly. There was no doubting the riders' intentions now and, raising their rifles, they began to return fire. A couple of men fell from their horses. Other horses reared. The riders slowed for an instant, but then tore on, careering down the main street of town, whooping and shouting and firing at random. Glass shattered near Snelgrove's head and he felt blood running down his face where he had been cut by a shard of glass. He ran out into the street in order to continue firing at the disappearing riders before turning to look for his deputy.

'Are you OK, Drabble?' he called. The figure of the deputy appeared from behind a stanchion.

'Yeah,' he replied. He glanced at three bodies lying in the dust. Another man was on his knees groaning. In an instant the sheriff had strode across to him and seized him by the collar.

'What the hell is goin' on?' he snapped.

As if by way of reply there came a shattering explosion from the other end of town. Snelgrove looked up, startled, to see a cloud of dense black smoke spiralling into the air.

'Come on!' he shouted at Drabble. 'Looks like this is only a diversion. I figure they've blown up the bank.'

Leaving the man where he kneeled in pain, blood oozing from a wound in his side, they started running in the direction of the explosion. The centre of town was strangely deserted where people had taken shelter in the buildings and the riders had carried on towards the bank. It was hard to see clearly what was happening as dust and smoke filled the air. An expanding flower of red and yellow flame rose into the sky and from the roof of the saloon someone was firing down. Snelgrove's first thought was that it was one of the gunmen, but he quickly realized the shots were being aimed at the bank, so it must be one of the townsmen who had taken to arms. The fire crackled and snapped and it seemed only a matter of time before it spread to other buildings and threatened the whole town. A man Snelgrove recognized as one of the bank clerks suddenly appeared in the doorway of the bank and began running, but he didn't get far as a couple of bullets hit him in the back and he went tumbling head over heels like a jackrabbit. Most of the riders seemed to have disappeared although Snelgrove could hear shooting in the distance. He continued running and had almost reached the bank when three men burst through the doorway and began running hard towards another group of riders who held horses by their reins. The men sprang into leather and the whole group began to ride away. Snelgrove raised his rifle and opened fire, but they had a clear start. They tore away and were quickly out of range. His instinct was to find his horse and give pursuit, but he quickly realized that the priority was to put out the fire and stop it spreading.

Already some of the citizens had emerged from cover and were taking steps to douse the flames. Signalling to Drabble to follow his example, he rushed to the nearest water trough and, filling one of the buckets which had appeared, rushed to the spot where the fire was fiercest. It seemed a hopeless task at first, but as more people emerged and joined in the struggle, the flames gradually began to diminish. Above the noise and bustle Snelgrove detected a creaking sound.

'Move away!' he shouted.

Responding to his command, the people nearby leaped clear in the nick of time as one wall of the building swayed and then toppled to the ground, filling the air with clouds of dust and debris and sending showers of sparks drifting like fireflies through the atmosphere. Once they had recovered from the shock, the townsfolk rejoined the battle with the blaze. There wasn't much else they could do, but continue to pour water over the lingering flames. Occasionally someone would give a start and look about, listening for the sound of hoofs or the rattle of gunfire, but it was fairly apparent that the riders had gone. It was clear to Snelgrove that the bank had been their target, and they had been successful. He would have to wait to see how much they had got away with. It was soon evident that, in addition to the bank clerk who had taken a bullet in the back, the bank manager had been injured too, but not seriously. A second clerk was shaken but unhurt. There wasn't a lot to be done except continue to pour buckets of water over the lingering flames and smouldering ruins. A few people were beating at the flames with blankets. A pall of smoke and ash hung over the town, but at least the townsfolk had managed to put out the fire and prevent an even bigger disaster.

When he was satisfied that things were more or less under control, Snelgrove made his way over to where a small knot of people were gathered around the bank manager. He had suffered a blow to the head from the butt of a six-gun, but a big bump and a raging headache seemed to be the worst consequences of his ordeal.

'How much did they get?' Snelgrove asked. The bank manager gave him a dazed look.

'I don't know yet,' he said. 'I haven't had a chance to check. But there was more than twenty thousand dollars in notes as well as a small supply of gold coins in the safe they blew.' The sheriff patted him on the shoulder.

'Don't worry,' he said. 'I'll make a point of gettin' it back again.'

'It's not so much the money,' the manager said, 'I understand they shot and killed poor Donaldson.'

'They'll pay for that as well.'

Snelgrove returned to the group of people dousing the last embers of the fire outside. They looked up at his approach and it seemed to him there was a questioning look in their eyes. He felt their pain and confusion. Nothing like the events that had just occurred had happened while he had been sheriff and he felt almost as shocked as they did. What was more, he took it as a personal affront. He was responsible for the maintenance of law and order in the town and in the county. He prided himself on the job he had done. Desolation Wells, despite its name, was the sort of place people could settle and put down roots, the sort of place that had a future; that had now been undermined, but he meant to restore the peoples' faith in their town and in himself. Lost in his thoughts, he didn't at first hear the voice of his deputy.

'Who do you think did this?' He turned to Drabble.

'I don't know, but we're soon gonna find out.' There was a moment's pause before Drabble replied.

'First Dwayne Oliver and now this. Do you reckon there could be a connection?'

'Not if you're askin' whether I think this was some sort of revenge attack. It's too much of a coincidence. All the same, I think it's likely Oliver was linked to those varmints. Maybe he was just another member of the gang.'

'You said somethin' about Oliver bein' too close to Desolation Wells for comfort. Well, it looks like you were right.'

Snelgrove took a long look at the scene of destruction. The smell of burning hung heavy in the air and his eyes smarted. His cheek hurt where it had been gashed by the splinter of glass. In his depleted state, Drabble's comments worked like a cold blade. Could he have done something to avoid the trouble happening?

'First things first,' he said. 'Once we've got this place lookin' somethin' like itself again, we can set about bringin' those vermin to justice. And I think our first stop might be the *Barbed S*.'

'The *Barbed S*?'

'That's where Oliver and his compadres seem to come from in the first place. Remember, they tracked Westoe to Desolation Wells.'

'Do you know where the *Barbed S* is?'

Snelgrove glanced down the length of the street away from the fire. A rider was coming towards them and the sheriff's face creased in a grim smile as he watched his approach.

'Nope,' he replied, 'but here comes someone who can show us the way.'

Drabble looked in the same direction, but didn't recognize the newcomer. 'Who is it?' he asked.

'It's Barnet. You know, the one I set off with to try and find Westoe. Well, it looks like he's finally abandoned the enterprise.'

* * *

It didn't sit easy with Westoe to spend so much time having to stay in bed and take it easy. He was encouraged by Leonae to lie face down in order to ease the pressure on his back. Each morning she came in and changed the dressing, reappearing at certain times to bring him food. Sometimes the door to his room was left open and he could hear desultory scraps of conversation drifting through. It seemed the trading post was doing a decent business. It made him feel more guilty that she was having to give time and attention to him as well. He expected Ben Howe to put in an appearance, but when some time had passed and he hadn't showed up, he raised the matter with Leonae.

'Ben's gone to take a look at what's left of his cabin and livestock,' she said. 'You know it got burned down?'

'Yeah. I feel real bad about it. Maybe if I'd stayed around it wouldn't have happened.'

'Ben told me about what occurred. You can't blame yourself. It was thanks to you he managed to fight off that first attack.'

Westoe eyed her closely. It was clear from the lines on her tightly drawn face that life wasn't easy for her. Despite that, she was still a good looking woman. There was something he wanted to broach with her, but he was hesitant.

'Something's goin' on around here,' he said, 'and I think I've got a pretty good idea what it is.' She turned her head to look at him. 'I've been thinkin' about something Ben said,' he continued. 'He told me that after I'd left, he had a visit from Holden Stroup. He told him what had happened. It seems it was his son that I shot. The strange thing was that Stroup wasn't angry. He just listened to what Ben said and then took the body back with him. It was a couple of days afterwards that his place got burnt out. So who was responsible? Apparently it wasn't Holden Stroup.' He paused to observe the effect of his words. He expected her to be surprised or puzzled, but her expression did not indicate that she was.

'There's somethin' else,' he went on. 'What Ben told me cleared up the mystery of who followed me to Desolation Wells. It can only have been riders from the *Barbed S*, but if Holden Stroup took the news that I was the one responsible for his son's death so calmly, then why would he have arranged for me to be tracked down? It doesn't add up.'

He looked again at Leonae. Her expression was tense and he thought he read pain in her limpid grey eyes. In the few moments of silence that filled the room the calling of a bird came faintly through the open window. Then she spoke.

'What you say doesn't surprise me. Holden Stroup is a good man. But that doesn't apply to his sons. At least it doesn't apply to Rafe. The one you shot, Eben, wasn't such a bad boy. It was Rafe who led him on. I don't like to criticize anybody and we were hopin' our suspicions weren't justified, but there can be no doubt now about the way things stand. All the bad things that have been happenin' round these parts are down to Rafe Stroup. It started in a small way, but it's just been gettin' worse and worse. I used to figure Rafe had just got himself in with some bad men and he would change, but now I see he's the main culprit.'

Westoe was struggling to understand the ramifications of what Leonae was telling him. He suddenly thought of the gravestone he had come across, marked with the name of Sean Bowman.

'Maybe you're right about those people following you being from the *Barbed S*,' she continued, 'but what's your evidence?'

'I saw the brand on their horses.'

'That doesn't have to mean anything. Maybe it wasn't Holden Stoup who set them on you, but Rafe. He was probably the one behind the shootout. It's just about certain he's the one responsible for burning down Ben Howe's cabin.'

'What for? Why would he do it?'

'Burn down the cabin? There's no real answer to that question. Just for the hell of it I guess. Maybe he's got some plan of his own, but who can figure out someone like that.'

'I still don't see why he would bother with me.'

'Wait a minute,' she replied. 'Didn't you say that the young man you spoke to at the *Barbed S* mentioned that Barnet, the foreman, was away on business?'

'Lucas Bunch,' Westoe interjected.

'Yes. I couldn't think of his name. It could be that Holden set Barnet to follow you to try and find out just exactly what happened when Eben got killed and confirm Ben Howe's account. Rafe could have got wind of it and arranged to have one of his cronies ride along just to make sure there were no complications. After all, he stands to inherit the ranch.'

Westoe was thinking hard, considering what she had said. It was all somewhat confusing, but it began to make a kind of sense. He looked across at Leonae and as they exchanged glances, he suddenly felt a new emotion. He felt protective and had an urge to put his arms around her, but before he could do anything she rose to her feet.

'I think that's enough for now,' she said. 'I want you to concentrate on getting well. All this can wait for now. I shouldn't be burdening you with problems that are none of your own.'

'Look at me,' he replied. 'I'd say they were very much my concern. Besides, I'm the one who raised the whole matter.'

He wanted to ask about Sean Bowman, but didn't see how he could do so and before he could say anything further she had taken the tray on which she had brought his food and moved to the doorway.

'Get some rest,' she said. 'I'll come back later.'

She went through to the store, closing the door gently behind her. He lay still, looking after her before eventually turning over on his side. Although he had already learned much that he needed to know, he still determined to pay another visit to the *Barbed S*. He wanted to see for himself what sort of an operation Holden Stroup ran. Lucas Bunch had seemed a decent sort. Would the acting foreman Sumter turn out the same? Or would the *Barbed S* cowboys turn out to be but a bunch of gunslicks in disguise? There was another reason too. If Rafe Stroup was the villain Leonae suspected him to be, a stop had to be put to his activities. He needed to be brought to justice. That couldn't happen till his hideout was discovered. There was yet one other thing. Although he could not have avoided it, he felt a need to apologize to Holden Stroup for shooting his son.

* * *

In stark contrast to the mood of general despondency that hung over the devastated town of Desolation Wells in the days following the bank robbery, Rafe Stroup and his gang of desperadoes were having a grand time celebrating their success. They rode hard to get back to their hideout, but once they arrived the festivities began. That night they let loose. Light spilled from the buildings, fires blazed and liquor flowed freely. The raucous sound of voices rose into the night air as the men shouted and argued, whooped and called out the old rebel yell. At intervals gunfire echoed from the surrounding hills as the owlhoots fired into the air. Occasionally a drunken fight would erupt, but it was all part of the fun.

Rafe could afford to congratulate himself. The success of the operation confirmed his status as leader of the gang and the general feeling was that the Bronco Boys were really on their way. There was only one slight cloud on his horizon, and that was the absence of

Dwayne Oliver. The gunslinger was as close to a confidante as he had ever known, but that wasn't saying much. There was always Skinner to take his place. No, he was more concerned that none of the three who had set off to trail the stranger involved in the shooting of his brother had returned. They should have been back by now. Had Oliver dealt with him? He would certainly have expected to see Barnet back at the ranch. However, he wasn't going to lose any sleep over the matter. The Bronco Boys were ready for more. The attack on the bank seemed only to have whetted their appetite, which was just as well because Rafe had already started to plan for their next escapade. Forgetting Oliver, he took advantage of a slight lull in the proceedings to call Skinner over. The man had drunk too much, but that didn't matter. Rafe's only use for him was as a receptacle for his own ideas.

'The boys are enjoyin' themselves,' he began.

'They sure are,' Skinner replied.

'They did well, but I can tell they're ready for more.' Skinner looked up at him.

'Yeah. Sure.' He sought for more words to say, but couldn't find them.

'Aren't you interested in what I got planned next?' Rafe said.

'Sure. The boys are ready. Sure. So am I.'

A smile like a rictus spread across Rafe's features. 'Then I'll tell you. As soon as the boys have got over their celebrations, we're gonna hit the *Barbed S*.' Skinner's expression was blank as he looked at Rafe through bleary eyes.

'The *Barbed S*,' he said. Somewhere in his throbbing head a muddled thought was trying to materialize. 'The *Barbed S* . . . but isn't . . . ' He didn't get any further as Rafe's voice cut in.

'Yes, the *Barbed S*. That ranch should belong to me. The old man isn't fit to run it no more. He always preferred Eben to me. Well, Eben ain't around anymore and I don't intend waitin' any longer for the old man to croak. I'm gonna take what is mine and then I'm gonna take over all the other ranches. You'll see. Pretty soon this whole territory is gonna belong to me. I got the money now. If they don't want to sell, we'll run 'em out.' He broke into a shrill laugh. 'Hell, I ain't gonna waste any money. We'll just drive them out anyway. Let the boys have some fun.'

Skinner was confused, but the sound of Rafe's laughter coupled with the suggestion of having some fun seemed to register with him.

'Yeah. We're gonna have fun. We're takin' over. Ain't nothin' gonna stop the Bronco Boys.'

5

The trail from Bowman's Store and trading post was familiar to Westoe because it was the second time he had ridden it, but it still felt strange. He put it down to the fact that he had only just recovered from his wound. Leonae was probably right when she said he should wait a little longer, but he was restless and keen to get back into action. Ben Howe had volunteered to accompany him, but he had pointed out that for him to do so would obviate the point of the exercise. He wanted to get an insider's view of how things were at the *Barbed S*, and that meant trying for a job. It was with reluctance that the oldster had agreed to remain behind. His trip to the burnt-out cabin had proved not entirely unsuccessful. He had managed to recover a few articles and papers, but it was no recompense for what he had lost, and he still did not know what had become of his meagre herd of cattle.

'You can stay here at the trading post as long as you want,' Leonae said. 'It'll be good to have you around. I reckon I could certainly use some help.'

'Once this business is over,' Westoe said, 'we'll see about rebuildin' that spread of yours.'

If Westoe had been more alert, he might have read something in Leonae's words to the oldster, but his mind was occupied with getting to the *Barbed S*. Even so, he couldn't mistake the anxious look in her eyes as he made to leave, nor his own feelings as he rode away.

'I'll be back,' he had said, and he couldn't have explained just what his own words signified.

He rode at a good pace, though mindful of the buckskin, and it didn't seem to take so long till the *Barbed S* ranch house hove into view. As he rode into the yard he looked out for Lucas

Bunch, but this time the youngster did not appear. He also kept a wary eye open for Rafe Stroup. He knew he was taking a chance, but Lucas had said he was often away from the ranch and Rafe would probably not recognize him even if he was there. He wasn't sure of the best way to proceed, but the issue was taken out of his hands when the door opened and a middle-aged man appeared on the veranda.

'I saw you ride up,' he said. He looked Westoe up and down. 'Don't get too many visitors,' he said. 'Maybe you'd better state your business.'

'I was hopin' to speak to Mr Stroup,' Westoe replied.

'Which one? I'm Holden Stroup. I'm the owner of the *Barbed S*.'

'Then it's you I want to see.' Stroup looked closely into Westoe's face.

'This isn't anythin' to do with my son Rafe?' he said. Westoe hesitated, but only for a moment.

'Nope,' he replied. 'It ain't anythin' much. I just rode out here to see if there might be a job goin'.'

Before Stroup could reply, a voice called out from inside. 'Everythin' OK, Mr Stroup?'

'Sure, everything's fine,' Stroup replied. He turned back to Westoe.

'Have you ever worked on a ranch before?' he asked.

'I've got plenty of experience.'

Stroup continued to look closely at Westoe. 'Why the *Barbed S?*' he said.

'I'm told it's one of the biggest spreads around. No other reason.'

Stroup thought for a moment. 'Well,' he said, 'I guess you've come to the right place. As a matter of fact, I could use an extra hand. It'll be hard work, though.'

'That suits me,' Westoe replied. Stroup nodded.

'Why don't you mosey on over to the bunk house,' he said, 'and have a word with my acting foreman, Jack Sumter. If he isn't back yet, just wait. He'll be along.' He made to go inside and then turned back again.

'You got a name?' he said. 'I reckon I might as well know it.'

For a moment Westoe thought of giving a false name, but then decided there was nothing to be gained by doing so.

'Chet Westoe,' he replied. 'And thanks for the job.'

'You might not be sayin' that when you've been here for a day or two. Like I said, you'll be earnin' your keep. Sumter can fill you in with all the details, but be ready to start right away tomorrow.'

Westoe nodded in acknowledgement and then stepped from the veranda as the door to the ranch house closed behind Stroup. His first impressions of the owner of the *Barbed S* were good. He would find out soon enough whether they were justified.

He soon found out that Stroup wasn't exaggerating when he said the work would be hard. The first morning he was instructed to ride as far as the border of the range in order to locate some cattle which had drifted and throw them back onto the *Barbed S* range. As he rode he searched the landscape, familiarizing himself with its features, discovering, among other things, patches of loco weed from which cattle had to be driven and a cow mired in a bog hole which he roped and pulled back to dry ground. The section of range he had been sent to patrol seemed to be of poorer quality and he guessed this was why no effort had been made to fence it off.

The next day he rode down into the draws and coulees and rousted out some cattle which had strayed, working hard to prevent them circling and getting back in. It was a tough job; a couple of old bulls kept trying to lead the others back, but he rode them tight. The brush was quite dense in places and he had to be very careful to avoid thorns and branches from tearing at his face, using his arms, legs and shoulders to help shield him. It reminded him of the *brasada* he had worked one time back in Texas. After a time he had a group of more than a dozen cattle. He had been working hard all day and was considering whether to carry on any further when he saw a rider approaching. As the man got closer, he started to wave his hat and then Westoe recognized him. It was Lucas Bunch. The youngster rode up and almost jumped from the saddle.

'Mr Westoe,' he shouted. 'I heard someone new had been taken on. I was kinda hopin' it might be you.'

'Howdy,' Westoe said, holding out his hand. 'It's sure good to see you again.'

'It's been a few days now. I figured you must have changed your mind about gettin' a job with the *Barbed S*.'

'Let's just say somethin' happened to delay me.'

'I'm headin' back,' Bunch said. 'How about we ride in together?' Westoe cast an eye on the cattle.

'I'm just figurin' what to do with these critters,' he said. 'If I leave 'em, they'll probably head back into the brush.'

'Let me give you a hand. We can drive 'em at least part way back to the ranch house.'

'That sounds like a good idea,' Westoe said.

It was an easy enough matter for the two of them, and as they rode Westoe took advantage of the opportunity to ask the youngster a few questions.

'There should be more of 'em,' he commented. 'There's plenty of sign, but too many of those draws are empty.'

'Well, that wouldn't be too surprisin',' Bunch replied. 'From what the boys have been sayin', it seems like quite a few of the cattle have been disappearin'.'

'Cattle rustling?' Westoe queried. 'Has anybody got an idea who might be behind it?'

'Not that I know. As far as I'm aware, Mr Stroup is on good relations with all his neighbours.'

'Have any of them been losin' stock?'

'I think so, but you'd best have a word with Mr Sumter or Mr Barnet when he gets back.'

'Where is Barnet? It's kind of unusual for the foreman to be away, isn't it?' The youngster shrugged and they rode on in silence till Westoe attempted another approach.

'I think you said Mr Stroup had two sons. Did neither of them show any interest in the runnin' of the ranch?'

'Nope. And now Eben's dead. We never did see too much of Rafe. In fact, we ain't seen him since the day you met him.'

'Only briefly.'

'Yeah, but even so I reckon you could see what sort he is. As for me, I was warned to give him a wide berth and that's just exactly the way I've been playin' it.'

'Where does Rafe get to when he's away?' Again the youngster shrugged.

'I don't know and I don't care. As far as I'm concerned, the more he ain't here, the better it is for everyone.'

They rode slowly, occasionally spurring forward to haze in any of the cattle that seemed inclined to wander. Suddenly Westoe had an inspiration.

'Does the name Sean Bowman mean anythin' to you? His mother runs a trading post not too far from here. Maybe you know it.'

'Sure I know it. And I knew Sean Bowman. Not personally, you understand. Only because he used to hang out with Rafe from time to time. In fact, they were real friendly for a while. Then he vanished from sight and I only heard later that he'd been killed.'

'Killed? Why, what happened.'

'You sure seem to be interested in all this,' Bunch replied. 'Sorry, I can't really help. There was a rumour he'd got into some sort of fight. I didn't really pay it a lot of attention. It's only because you ask that I remember anythin' about it now.'

'Sorry. None of it's any of my business either. I guess we're just shootin' the breeze.'

All the while Westoe had been observing the terrain, matching it against his first impressions, and he realized they were getting quite close to the ranch.

'What do you reckon?' he said to the youngster. 'Do you think we've brought these critters far enough?'

'I guess so.'

'Then I figure we can leave 'em right here till it's time for the roundup.'

They rode the rest of the way in silence and the sun was touching the horizon when they pulled up outside the stables.

'I'm sure lookin' forward to some grub,' the youngster said.

'Yeah. Ridin' the range makes you feel kinda hungry. Best see to these horses first,' Westoe replied. Bunch walked over and ran his hands along the buckskin's flanks.

'I started off as wrangler so I know a good horse when I see one,' he said. 'That sure is a fine animal.'

'Yeah, though she's more of a range

horse than a cow horse.'

'Once we start up the trail, you can pick your own string.'

Westoe didn't reply. He had got himself a job with the *Barbed S* for purely pragmatic reasons — to find out something more about the set-up. Despite the hard nature of the work, he found he had enjoyed it. He had also begun to feel an unexpected sense of obligation. Leaving everything else that had happened out of account, did he still owe Stroup something? He wasn't sure whether there was much else to be learned. Bearing in mind that Barnet might arrive at any time, did it make any sense to remain much longer? He had almost decided the time had come to make himself scarce, but now he wasn't so sure. If Barnet turned up, would he recognize him? He had only a vague impression of the man, gained from observing his pursuers through his field-glasses. Presumably Barnet's image of him, assuming he had one, had been gained the same way. It wasn't his style to cut and run. Maybe he should stick around after all, at least for a time, and see how things worked out.

In the days following his encounter with Bunch, Westoe saw little of the youngster. He worked hard at the tasks he had been assigned, setting off early and returning late. The evenings passed without incident. He got on with the rest of the men he met and joined them a time or two in a game of cards. They confirmed the impression Stroup and Sumter had made; that they were a decent bunch and the *Barbed S* a well-run outfit. But then, there was Rafe Stroup — he didn't seem to fit into the picture.

The morning of the third day passed and towards noon he was about to have a break when he stopped in his tracks. The buckskin's ears were lifted and it was clear something was disturbing her. He looked around. The range was empty and still except for the droning of flies, but it seemed to him there was something ominous in the atmosphere. He untied his bandana and mopped his face. The air hung heavy, as if a storm was brewing, but the sky was blue and cloudless.

'What is it, old girl?' he said to the horse.

It edged sideways and stamped its hoof. Through the dancing, shimmering haze Westoe's eyes scanned the horizon. He licked his lips and unconsciously bent forwards, listening intently, and presently his ears picked up a low rumbling sound. It grew louder, like the gathering thrum of a railroad train or the reverberation of thunder. For a few moments he was confused and then he realized what it was: the drumming of horses' hoofs. He peered even harder into the distance and caught sight of a dark cloud which seemed to hover on the horizon, but it wasn't a cloud; it was the dust raised by a mass of galloping horsemen and it was heading towards the *Barbed S*. He had no idea what it all portended, but he knew it couldn't be anything good.

In an instant he was in the saddle and headed in the same direction, but coming at the ranch house from a different angle. As he rode, he kept looking in the direction of the as yet unseen horsemen, and soon had his first glimpse of them. It was hard to tell how many there were, but there were plenty. They had split into two groups of more or less equal sizes, accompanied by others who had fallen back and become strung out behind. Who were they? They still had some way to go before they reached the ranch house, but as they converged they caught sight of him and a few shots began to ring out. He spurred his horse harder and was rapidly gaining on them. His intention was to reach the ranch house ahead of them, not to give warning because he realized the advancing horde must have been seen, but to play his part in the defence of the *Barbed S*. He was ahead of the pack and for the first time became concerned about what sort of reception he might receive. If they didn't recognize him, he was likely to be met by a hail of bullets. There was no time for consideration. He would just have to take his chances.

Some shots were still being fired in his direction, but he was too far away. They carried no real threat and soon he was even further ahead and out of range. The buckskin hurtled on, foam flying from its nostrils, but the distance to the ranch house seemed to have grown since he had set off earlier that day. A dip in the land put him out of sight of the attacking horde, although he could still hear the drum of their horses' hoofs. How many men could Holden Stroup muster? He wasn't sure about the numbers, but it was certain that a good number of them would be out working on various parts of the range. How many would volunteer to come back and put up a fight? There was no way of knowing and he settled himself to carry on riding as hard as he dared, trusting that the buckskin wouldn't put its hoof in a gopher hole and send him flying.

After what seemed an age the ranch house appeared ahead of him. It had a curious look as though it was deserted, and he guessed that Stroup had already placed his men ready for battle. He could only hope and pray that he would be recognized. The buckskin tore into the yard and before it had stopped he had already drawn his rifle from its scabbard and launched himself from the saddle. He smacked the horse hard on its rump and it carried on in the direction of the corral. He turned to the veranda, shouting 'It's me, Westoe.' In response the ranch house door swung open and he dashed inside. His eyes quickly took in the scene. A man had been placed at each window, among whom he recognized Sumter as well as Stroup himself.

'You were damned lucky you weren't shot,' Stroup snapped.

'Never mind that. Where do you want me?'

'We're short of men upstairs. Take one of the front rooms.'

'One of the men rode in with the news that a bunch of riders were headed this way, but he only saw them from a distance. Did you get a chance to see who they are?' Sumter said.

'Nope, but they're sure lookin' for trouble.'

As the sound of the approaching riders began to swell, he ran for the stairs. It was the first time he had been in the ranch house since his initial conversation with Stroup, but there was no time for observation as the first crack of rifle fire boomed from outside. At the top of the landing there was an open door and he ran through. The room seemed to be some sort of study with books on shelves and a long window overlooking the yard. He peered out as the riders came into view, firing as they came.

There was a response from inside the ranch house and then the yard erupted into a thunder of noise. The attackers were firing rapidly, but it was a random volley. Smoke began to billow through the yard, and through it Westoe could now see them still coming forward, but reining in their horses, apparently surprised by the response. Some of them began to turn back and Westoe took advantage of the confusion, firing into the melee of horses and riders. For a few minutes Holden Stroup's men held an advantage, but the situation was soon resolved as the attackers drew back and began to spread out and take cover. Bullets now slapped into the walls of the ranch house and Westoe pulled back his head as lead ripped into the window shutter, showering him with sharp splinters of wood. He pumped bullets into his rifle and levered off another round. He couldn't see exactly what was happening because of the smoke, but several bodies were lying on the ground. After a rapid exchange of shots the firing became more sporadic.

'Everybody OK?' a voice yelled.

There was an answering chorus in the affirmative.

He took another look out the window. Apart from the dead and dying in the yard, he could see no sign of anybody. A stray horse crossed his line of vision and wandered away. He strained his eyes to see if he could discern any markings, but it was too far away and quickly gone. Its presence gave him an idea and he moved quickly to the landing, looking about for a way up to the roof. There was a skylight and he quickly fetched a chair in order to reach up to it. With some effort, he succeeded in forcing it open and then poked his head above the tiles. He was at the back of the building and he was protected from the view of anyone at the front by a chimney. He climbed out and lay flat, surveying the scene. The first thing he saw was that some of the attackers were making their way under cover of the outbuildings to the rear of the ranch house, obviously aiming to surround it. They weren't being exceptionally careful and he was strongly tempted to take a shot with his Army Colt, but he resisted the temptation. Then he saw something which really made him start. Away to the right and out of range, a man appeared directing some of his companions. He was some distance away, but Westoe thought he recognized Rafe Stroup. He had only run across Rafe once, the first time he had visited the *Barbed S* and met Bunch, but he felt certain it was him. It wasn't just what he could discern of the man's features. The clothes he wore were the same and there was a certain angularity to his figure. If it was Rafe Stroup, then the mystery of who was attacking the *Barbed S* only deepened. Why would Rafe lay siege to his own father's ranch? It didn't make sense. Nonetheless, he was sure it was Rafe. As he peered closely, the man disappeared again. Westoe had seen enough. He began to slither back towards the sky-light in the same moment that a rifle cracked and a bullet went singing over his head from someone who must have caught sight of him. Supporting himself on his arms, he dropped to the floor of the landing before making his way to the stairwell.

'They're circling us,' he rapped.

'Hell, that doesn't sound too good,' Stroup replied

He was just about to tell him what he else he had seen from the rooftop when there came a rattle of gunfire from outside.

'Get back to your places, men!' Stroup shouted.

He didn't really need to give the command because most of them were still at their positions by the windows. This time, however, the shooting came not just from the front of the ranch house, where it was still concentrated, but from all sides; a furious cannonade that seemed to shake the house to its foundations. Bullets thudded into the walls of the building and began to ricochet around the interior, shattering objects to smithereens. Westoe had taken up his position by the upstairs study window and was firing as quickly as he could when he felt a sharp pain and staggered back, blood running down his cheek. It wasn't serious and, ignoring it, he turned back and began pumping bullets into the yard outside, firing where he saw flame. He could hear the rattle of gunfire towards the back of the building and realized that some of the men had changed positions to meet the challenge there, but he doubted whether they would be able to hold the attackers off for much longer. A further crescendo of gunfire came from that direction and then, unexpectedly, there was a lull. He took the opportunity to peer out of the window and in the distance he thought he could discern a cloud of dust. At the same time, some of the attackers who were just out of range emerged from their places of concealment and moved towards their horses. In a few moments they had mounted and were riding away. From the back of the houses someone began to shout:

'I think they're callin' it a day!'

He couldn't understand what was happening Then, after a few moments, he heard the sound of hoof beats and his heart sank. If Rafe was about to bring up more of his men, they were doomed. The riders were getting closer. There were about five or six of them and they were coming up fast, seemingly oblivious of danger. Shots began to ring out, but it was impossible to say who was doing the shooting. He took the chance of exposing himself to gunfire in order to get a better look and when he recognized the slim figure of Bunch, he realized that they were not more of Rafe's gunslicks, but some of the *Barbed S* men who had been absent when the attack began. As if that wasn't enough, a moment later he almost rubbed his eyes in astonishment. Among the other riders he recognized two people he would never have expected to see again. One was the oldster, Ben Howe, and the other was the sheriff of Desolation Wells. He then realized that it was because of these two men that the gunslicks were moving away. He was expecting them to ride straight into the yard, but when they were a little distance they came to a halt, dismounted and took shelter. A fresh fusillade of shots rang out as a small group of horsemen came into view from around the side of the ranch house, spurring their horses in their haste to get away. Raising his rifle, he directed his fire towards them, but they had veered away and were already out of range. The firing from immediately in front of him had dwindled to almost nothing and after a few more minutes it died away altogether. In contrast to the previous cacophony of noise, the ensuing quiet was almost palpable.

Westoe remained at his post, watching for any further signs of activity, but nothing was happening. Then he heard movement from down below and the sound of the ranch house door being opened. A few moments later, Stroup emerged. It seemed to Westoe that he was taking a chance and he lifted his rifle to cover him. Stroup walked steadily forward till he stood out in the yard, fully exposed to a shot from any gunman who still remained. Tension hung in the air. Westoe made to leave his post and make his way downstairs, but then decided against it, thinking that he would do better to remain where he was. He stood with his rifle raised, his eyes searching the scene for any sign of movement which might betray the presence of a lingering gunslick. Unexpectedly, a voice rang out:

'Get back inside! Don't take any chances!'

By way of reply, Stroup raised his own voice, but it was to ask another question.

'Rafe!' he yelled. 'I know it's you. I don't know why and I don't care. If you're still there, come out of hidin'.

I'm tellin' my men not to shoot anymore. I guarantee your safety. Only tell me why. I need to know what reason you had to do this.'

The echoes of his voice died away, but there was no reply; only the soughing of the wind and the snicker of a horse. The seconds ticked by and seemed to extend into infinity. Then Stroup shouted again.

'Rafe. I'm still your father. You're still my son. Come back to me and whatever it is, we can work it out.'

There was no response. Presently some people emerged from the ranch house at the same time as other figures — Bunch and the sheriff among them — came into view from where they had taken cover. Stroup raised his arms towards the heavens and then seemed momentarily to totter as Sumter came up behind him and placed a hand on his shoulder. Stroup's head sank to his breast and it seemed to Westoe that a shudder shook him before he partly turned and let the deputy foreman lead him back towards the ranch house.

Westoe slowly lowered his rifle. Among all the other thoughts and emotions which were running through his brain, the dominant feeling was one of relief that he was spared the responsibility of having to tell Stroup about Rafe's presence at the scene; whether Stroup realized that Rafe was responsible for the attack was another matter. He turned away from the window, becoming aware again of the cut to his face. For a second time he had been lucky. Footsteps passed on the landing and following the other defenders who had been positioned on the upper floor, he started to make his way downstairs when he suddenly remembered the sheriff. He couldn't imagine what Snelgrove was doing there, but the way he had made his exit from Desolation Wells wouldn't be likely to have endeared him to that representative of the law. The situation was complicated, but there was every chance that he might find himself under arrest.

Reaching the landing, he leaned out to see what was happening downstairs. Despite their success in beating off the attack, the atmosphere was muted. He could see Stroup standing a little apart, surrounded by a group of people. He seemed to have recovered something of his equilibrium. Westoe couldn't see the sheriff, but as he placed his foot on the first step of the stairs one of the men talking to Stroup, who had his back to him, turned and with a shock he recognized Barnet. What was more to the point was that Barnet clearly recognized him. He hesitated for just a moment and then turned back, making his way along the corridor to one of the rooms facing the back of the building. He looked out. There was nobody around. The stable building was not far off and he figured he could make it there without being seen. It was quite a long drop to the ground, but the room overlooked a grassy patch and he reckoned he could make a soft landing. The window had been shattered by flying bullets and he quickly knocked out the last few sharp splinters of glass before climbing over the window ledge and lowering himself as far as he could. For a moment he hung on and then released his grip. He hit the ground harder then he had expected, but nothing was broken. He picked himself up and was about to make his way to the stable door when he heard the whinny of a horse. He looked around, thinking hard of an excuse to explain his presence, when he suddenly breathed a huge sigh of relief. The whinny he had heard was from a riderless horse which, although it was standing at a little distance, he recognised as his own buckskin. It took only a few moments for him to reach it and whisper calming words into its ear. He swung himself into the saddle and, touching his spurs to its flanks, began to ride away from the ranch house.

He continued till darkness fell and

then made camp. He lifted the saddle from the buckskin and picketed the horse on a patch of grass. He built a fire and made coffee. He was feeling hungry, but the best he could manage was a few strips of jerky he kept in his saddlebags. When he had finished, he built himself a smoke and sat by the fire to try and think things through. He wasn't sure what to do next. One option was to make his way back to Leonae's store and trading post. He would do that eventually, but the time now was not ripe. He had unfinished business with Stroup and the *Barbed S*. He could go back there and take his chances. Snelgrove would surely have realized he was not guilty of premeditated murder. However, he couldn't be absolutely sure of that. What was Snelgrove doing there in the first place? Maybe it was to arrest him and take him back to Desolation Wells. That could explain the presence of Drabble. The more he thought about it, the more confused he became. A few other things were pretty clear, however. One was that Rafe Stroup was up to no good. Another was that he was riding with a bunch of desperados who were responsible for most of the wrongdoing that had been taking place recently. He finished the cigarette and threw the stub into the fire. As he did so, his horse snickered. He looked up at its shadowy outline and thought he detected a shimmer of movement. Getting quickly to his feet, he moved back into the shadows and drew his Colt .44.

He hadn't long to wait. After a few moments he heard the unmistakable soft tread of a boot and then a dim figure emerged from the bushes at the far side of the clearing. Although he was being furtive, the man wasn't making a lot of effort to be silent. He moved slowly forwards till he fell within range of the flickering firelight, then Westoe recognized his stooping figure. Holstering his revolver, he stepped forwards. The man looked up at his approach and his hand dropped towards his gun belt before he recognized Westoe in turn.

'Chet,' he said. 'It's me, Ben Howe.'

'You're lucky I didn't shoot,' Westoe replied. 'You were taking a big risk creeping up on me like that.' He paused and then they both broke into a laugh. 'Hell, what are you doin' here, you old coot?'

'What do you think? Lookin' for you, of course.' They briefly embraced and then Westoe drew the oldster towards the fire.

'I figure you could use some strong coffee,' he said.

While he made a fresh brew, the oldster brought up his horse. 'When I saw your camp-fire, I figured it must be you,' he said. 'All the same, I thought I'd better leave the roan at a distance.' Westoe poured the coffee into two tin mugs then proffered his sack of Bull Durham and they both lit up.

'You realize we're a sittin' target for any of those varmints who attacked the

Barbed S?' Howe commented.

'I'd be happy if they came,' Westoe replied. 'I'd welcome the chance to even the score a little.'

'Don't worry. You'll get it. They were talkin' about organizin' a posse to try and track 'em down when I left.'

'I still don't see what you were doin' ridin' in with the sheriff like that.'

'Yeah. I guess it would have been kinda unexpected.'

'Whatever it was, it saved the day. If you hadn't showed up, I reckon we would have been overrun.'

'Maybe. If so, it was probably the surprise element that did it.'

The oldster finished his coffee and Westoe poured him another. 'Go on, then,' he said. 'Tell me what you were doin' there.'

'There's not much to tell. After you left, I got to feelin' kinda guilty about lettin' you go.'

'You didn't let me go anywhere. It was my choice to ride to the *Barbed S*.'

'Miss Leonae was mighty worried

too,' Howe replied somewhat inconsequentially. 'Well, we were figurin' what we should do when Sheriff Snelgrove and his deputy turned up, together with the foreman of the *Barbed S*.'

'Barnet?'

'Yeah, that's him. Between them they'd cooked up some cockamamie story about you, but I soon put them right. I told them what happened at my place the day you came by. We told them a few other things, too. But we didn't need to try and explain too hard, because the sheriff had a few things to say as well.'

'Is he lookin' to take me in?' Westoe asked, but Howe ignored the question.

'Seems like there's been trouble in Desolation Wells too. There was a hold-up at the bank. Oh, yes. And one of the men you shot back there turned out to be some gunslinger by name of Dwayne Oliver. I figure that fact alone was enough to establish your credentials. Anyway, the upshot of it is that Snelgrove put two and two together and decided the time had come to visit the *Barbed S*. We were on our way when we heard the shootin'.'

When he had finished his account, he looked closely at Westoe in the dancing light of the flames. 'Is that why you lit out?' he asked. 'Because you figured Snelgrove had come to take you in?'

'That and a few other things. I needed time to think.'

'Well, there ain't much to think about now,' the oldster replied. 'After everythin' that's happened, I reckon we all know the way things stand.' Westoe inhaled deeply.

'What about Stroup?' he said. 'How is he?'

'I'd say he's been hit hard. He's tryin' to put a brave face on it, but he knows the score.'

'I figured that from the way he spoke up when the fight ended, tryin' to get through to Rafe.'

'A lot of folks around here have known the truth about Rafe for a long time. Maybe Stroup did too. Maybe he just didn't want to admit it. If he didn't, he sure does now.'

'Does he know I was the one shot Eben?'

'He knows the truth. You can't go blamin' yourself.' Westoe was quiet, thinking hard.

'I need to get back and tell him,' he said. 'I need to talk to him face to face.'

'You figure that would be the best thing, just at the moment while he's still feelin' raw?'

'Don't you?

'No I don't. I figure the best way would be to let the dust settle. But if that's the way you want to play it . . . '

'Why did you follow me here?'

'To try and stop you doin' anythin' foolish.'

'Like headin' back to the *Barbed S*?'

'I figure the thing to do would be for us both to head right back to the trading post. Believe me; Leonae would sure be pleased to see you.'

'Nothin' would suit me better. But I owe Stroup. I should have stuck around in the first place.'

Howe shrugged his shoulders. 'I think you're wrong,' he said, 'but if that's the way you feel . . . ' Again, he left his sentence unfinished. Westoe finished his coffee. The night was chilly and he threw a few more sticks on the fire.

'You're forgettin' somethin',' he said, as if there had been no break in the conversation.

'Oh yeah? And what's that?'

'I've got as big a stake in dealin' with Rafe and his gunslicks as anybody. Maybe more than some. If Snelgrove is goin' after them, I aim to be right alongside.'

In the firelight he could see the oldster grin.

'Now you're makin' sense,' he said. 'I reckon we can agree on that. I ain't forgot what they did to my cabin.'

* * *

Rafe Stroup was a lot of bad things, but he was no fool. He realized that when he and his men left the *Barbed S*, they left a trail anybody could follow. It didn't worry him. Even before they arrived back at their outlaw roost, he had a plan.

'You figure they'll come after us?' Skinner asked.

'Yup.' Skinner looked a little uneasy.

'Then maybe we should move on,' he said. Rafe looked him up and down with barely concealed contempt.

'"Move on",' he repeated. 'The Bronco Boys don't move on. They stand and fight.' Skinner couldn't help thinking that that was more than they had done at the ranch, but he didn't say anything.

'Don't worry,' Rafe continued. 'Just think for a moment. What have we got that they ain't got?' Skinner looked blank.

'Think man!' Rafe repeated. 'What was it gave us the edge when we hit that bank in Desolation Wells?'

Skinner racked his brains, but couldn't come up with an answer. He looked somewhat fearfully at Rafe.

'Dynamite!' Rafe shouted. 'We've got dynamite!' Skinner summoned up a faint grin, but he was still uncertain of what Rafe was driving at.

'Listen!' Rafe hissed. 'There's only one way in and out of this place, leastways as far as anybody else is concerned. They've got to come up by the key-hole pass. So, all we have to do is to place the dynamite there and then we'll blow 'em to kingdom come.'

A light dawned in Skinner's eyes. 'Yeah,' he muttered. Then a thought occurred to him and he thought he was being quite bright when he asked:

'Why didn't we use dynamite when we hit the *Barbed S*?'

Rafe's face twisted in rage. 'Are you stupid!' he yelled. 'I want the *Barbed S* for myself. It belongs to me. Why would I blow up my own ranch?' The enthusiasm faded from Skinner's eyes again.

'Oh yeah, sorry,' he mumbled.

'I don't know why I bother with you,'

Rafe snapped. His temper began to subside. He was feeling pleased with his plan and was not about to forego the opportunity of impressing Skinner further.

'And this is what else we do,' he said. 'Just in case anything goes wrong and any of 'em get through, we'll booby trap this place and blow 'em sky high again.'

'But . . . ' Skinner began. Rafe held up his hand.

'No buts,' he said. 'What does this place amount to after all? It's only a few old buildin's. We'll soon find someplace else, an even better place. The hideout don't matter. What matters is that the Bronco Boys carry on. What matters is that the Bronco Boys blaze their way clear across the territory and way beyond.' He paused. 'Besides,' he said, 'once we've dealt with anybody who dares come after us, we'll have the *Barbed S* for our new roost.'

The idea struck him as amusing and he began to laugh. In a few moments Skinner joined him. Their raucous merriment rang out across the valley, increasing in strength to a demented cackling.

6

The immediate consequences of the attack on the *Barbed S* were apparent to Westoe and Howe — almost the moment they reached *Barbed S* property they were met by a trio of horsemen.

'Just checkin',' one of them said. He turned to Howe. 'I recognize Westoe, but I ain't so sure about you.'

'If it weren't for me and Sheriff Snelgrove, you might not be here to argue the point,' Howe rejoined.

'It's OK,' the other man said. 'I can vouch for him.'

'Care to ride along with us?' Howe asked. There was no response to the oldster's attempt at sarcasm and they rode on.

'You seem kinda shirty,' Westoe commented.

'Guess maybe I am. I don't know.

They just kinda riled me some.'

'They're doin' a good job. Seems like Stroup ain't inclined to take any chances of those varmints payin' a return visit.'

They carried on in silence. As they got nearer the ranch house, Westoe could feel himself growing more tense. He had insisted on facing up to Stroup, but he didn't relish the prospect. He still had some concerns, too, about the attitude of Snelgrove and Barnet. If the sheriff was planning to go after Rafe and his gang of gunslicks, there was every likelihood he would still be there. His cogitations were interrupted by Howe's voice.

'You're sure about this? There's still time to turn back and head for the trading post.'

'I'm sure,' Westoe replied. He would rather have faced up to Rafe and his gang of hardcases single-handed, but he knew it was something he had to do.

It seemed to take a long time to cover the distance, but eventually the ranch house came into view. It seemed remarkably quiet after the previous day's events. The building, however, bore the scars of the battle. Its walls were pitted by bullets, most of the windows were smashed and there were bloodstains in the dirt of the yard and on the veranda. They rode up to the hitching rail and lowered themselves from the leather. As they were fastening their horses, the door of the ranch house opened and Stroup appeared with Barnet just behind him. Westoe and the oldster exchanged glances. As far as Westoe was concerned, it didn't look good. Stroup came forward to the top of the steps.

'Westoe,' he said, 'we were wonderin' where you were. We got to fearin' somethin' bad had happened.'

Westoe wondered if he meant the comment ironically, although Stroup gave every impression of being genuinely relieved to see him. Before Westoe could say anything in reply, Stroup continued:

'Come on in, the both of you.'

Barnet turned and went back through the door as Stroup ushered them in. When he stepped over the threshold, Westoe was taken aback to find Snelgrove was there too. The sheriff nodded in his direction and more or less repeated what Stroup had said.

'Howdy, Westoe. We were gettin' worried about you.' He turned his head towards Howe. 'I didn't get a chance to thank you for everythin'. Me and Drabble sure appreciate everythin' you've done.' Howe grinned.

'I guess we ain't finished yet,' he replied.

Stroup made his way to a cabinet and poured a couple of drinks, which he proffered to Westoe and Howe.

'We'd just filled our glasses. Won't you join us? Take a seat and make yourselves comfortable,' he said.

They sat down and took a swig of the whiskey. There was awkwardness in the air and Westoe wasn't sure how to proceed. He turned to the sheriff.

'I didn't expect to see you again,' he said. 'I guess I owe you an apology for the way I left.'

'No apologies required,' Snelgrove answered.

'I wouldn't normally . . . ' He didn't get any further as Stroup interrupted.

'There's no need to go on,' he said. 'The sheriff has informed us of what happened in Desolation Wells. In fact, I think you're the one who needs to be updated. Seems like a whole heap of things have been happening, but it's all pretty clear now.' He turned to Barnet. 'I don't think you've met my foreman. I think now might be a good time to remedy that situation.'

At Stroup's words, Barnet nodded and raised his glass. Westoe was feeling more confused than ever as he returned the compliment.

'I think some explanations are called for,' Stroup continued. 'I don't know just where to begin. Maybe I should start and then Barnet and the sheriff can take it on.' He took a drink from his own glass of whiskey and for a few moments seemed to hesitate. Then, gathering himself together, he started.

'To keep it as brief a possible, word was brought to me that my son Eben had been killed in a dispute with a passing stranger. Acting on what information I had, I decided to set Barnet the task of tracing the man with the intention of getting to the truth of the matter and if necessary, bringing him to justice. In the event it didn't turn out quite as I had envisaged, but that is another matter.'

'I never liked havin' Dwayne Oliver along,' Barnet said.

'No, it wasn't in the plan, but it happened.' Stroup turned to Westoe. 'The man they followed, of course, was you. I make my apologies right now for what happened in Desolation Wells.'

Westoe shook his head. He was feeling more and more uncomfortable and the burden of what he had to say was growing heavier with every word of

168

Stroup's. He couldn't concentrate on what was being said, even though it was of direct concern to him, and as the sheriff took up the story, he had to make an effort to quell his growing agitation. He felt someone's eyes resting on him and turned his head in Howe's direction. The oldster was looking at him with an expression which seemed to express an understanding of his discomfort. Westoe took another drink; time passed slowly and it was almost with a shock of surprise that he realized the voices had ceased. The silence was palpable by contrast, but it lasted for only a few moments before Stroup spoke again.

'So that's the whole story,' he said. 'I think we all realize now the truth of the matter.' He paused, obviously in some distress. 'I don't . . . I don't know what else to say. You'll understand . . . Rafe is still my son, despite everythin'. But I can't make excuses for him any more. What happened here yesterday . . . I was hoping against hope . . . I've tried to come up with an answer . . . ' He stopped and swallowed hard before turning to the sheriff. 'I realize what you have to do. Rafe and his gang have got to be stopped. I don't need to labour the point. We've already talked about it.' He turned to Westoe. 'We're organizing a posse to go after them. I guess you'd want to ride along too.'

Westoe glanced across at Howe again. The oldster's eyes still rested on him. He knew the time had come to say his piece. Putting his glass down on a table, he turned to Stroup.

'There's one thing you haven't mentioned,' he said, 'you or nobody else.' Stroup looked back at him with a puzzled expression. 'You haven't referred to the fact that it was me who killed Eben. You all know now what happened that day at Howe's cabin. I didn't do it deliberately, but nonetheless it was me who fired the shot that killed him. It was me who pulled the trigger.' He looked straight into Stroup's eyes. 'I don't know what to say,' he continued. 'I'm sorry it happened. I'm sorry for how I've hurt you.'

He was expecting some sort of reaction from Stroup, a sign of anger or grief. Instead the rancher just shook his head. Westoe couldn't read the expression on his features. The silence in the room was like a physical presence. When Stroup finally spoke, his tone was gentle.

'If what you say was true, I would forgive you. But it isn't true. You need have no regrets. You didn't kill Eben.' It was Westoe's turn to look puzzled. 'You carry a Winchester rifle, don't you?' Stroup continued. Westoe nodded his head in agreement. 'The bullet that killed Eben came from a Sharps.' There was a slight break in his voice before he added: 'The type of rifle favoured by Rafe.'

Westoe was struggling to take in what Stroup was telling him. 'How do you know that?' he managed to say.

'I took the body from Howe's place

and brought it home. I had the bullet removed. It was .50 calibre.' Westoe was thinking hard, trying to recall the details of the battle at Howe's cabin, and into his mind flashed the image of the man who was shooting from the shelter of the trees. Could it have been Rafe? Could he have fired the shot that killed Eben?

'Are you sure about this?' he managed to say. Stroup nodded his head.

'There isn't any doubt,' he replied. 'It was Rafe, not you, who killed Eben.'

The room was silent as the import of his words sank in. Then Stroup spoke again.

'Gentlemen, I think we all know what needs to be done and I don't see any sense in delay. It shouldn't be hard to follow those gunslicks. They must have left a trail a mile wide. So if you'll excuse me, I'm goin' to get ready.' He turned to Westoe. 'We've all just eaten. If you and Mr Howe are hungry, there's food over in the bunk house.'

He moved to the stairwell and began to mount the stairs. Once he had disappeared from sight the sheriff got to his feet.

'There wasn't any need to hightail it like you did,' he said. 'I figured you were probably innocent. Once I got to know it was Dwayne Oliver you shot, I knew it for certain. Those varmints holding up the bank only confirmed that somethin' was goin' on that needed dealin' with. Me and Drabble are sure glad we're all ridin' together now, even if the circumstances are maybe not how we'd like 'em to be.'

'You arrived in the nick of time,' Westoe replied. Just then Barnet came up.

'I reckon I owe you an apology,' he said. 'I should have guessed somethin' wasn't right when Oliver got involved. My only excuse is that I didn't realize just who he was.'

'I guess nobody was willin' to believe the truth about Rafe,' Snelgrove said. His words were greeted with an awkward silence which Howe finally broke.

'Let's you and me mosey over to the bunk house,' he said to Westoe. 'I don't know about you, but I figure I could do with somethin' to eat before we hit the trail.'

★ ★ ★

Rafe Stroup watched as fuses were placed in the dynamite. His men had been happy to booby-trap the entrance to their hidden valley, but some of them had expressed some concern about the idea of planting the black powder around the outlaw roost itself. A small group approached him and he put down the bottle of Forty-Rod from which he had been drinking.

'We ain't sure about this,' one of the men said. Rafe felt annoyance surge up in him but a glance from Skinner served to remind him that, for the moment at least, it might be sensible to curtail it.

'Hell,' he said, 'that stuff has been lyin' about for long enough. It could have gone off at any time. I never heard anyone complainin' about it before.'

'This is different. We didn't set it deliberately to go off.'

'We probably won't even need to set it off. It's just a precaution. If anyone comes after us, they won't get past here. They'll be blown all to hell.'

'Assumin' the stuff works.'

'It worked all right when we did the bank job.' He had struck the right note, but there were still a few grumbles before he continued.

'In any case, who says we have to hang about here? This is just temporary. I got plans. The bank job was just the start. I figure it's time we moved on to bigger things.'

Rafe realized that his stock, which was high after the bank robbery, had fallen as a result of the relative failure of the attack on the *Barbed S*. He knew he hadn't handled that episode particularly well. He had allowed himself to be spooked by the arrival of the additional *Barbed S* men, and now realized that there were a lot less of them than he had imagined. At the back of his mind was the thought that if his father and his *Barbed S* ranch-hands were to pursue him and get blown up in the process, the ranch would be his anyway. He wouldn't need a refuge in the hills. If it was likely ever to come in useful at some point in the future, he could rebuild it. It would take too much time and effort to try and explain these things to his men, however. Thinking wasn't their forte.

'OK,' he said, 'Have it your way. But let's get on with dynamitin' this place and make sure they never get any further.' Getting to his feet, he took some of the powder and, seizing a funnel from the hand of one of his interlocutors, began to pour it into a crack in the rock wall.

'Gimme that fuse,' he snapped. It was handed over to him and he corkscrewed it into place before tamping it all down.

'There, that's one more. Now get on and finish the job. Leave the worryin' to me.'

The men hesitated for just a moment and then, with some slight encouragement from Skinner, began to move away. Rafe glanced at his henchman.

'The quicker they come now the better,' he said. Skinner nodded.

'I figure we're ready for 'em,' he replied.

'The boys have still got to learn that we ain't dependent on stayin' around here for ever.'

Skinner didn't feel like arguing. His sympathies were in fact with those members of the gang who had expressed their antipathy to booby trapping their hideaway. Rafe took up the bottle of rot-gut whiskey and took another swig before letting his gaze wander across the valley floor and the narrow trail leading to the key-hole pass.

'They won't stand a chance,' he cackled. 'Hell, I wish they would come on right now.'

'I figure we won't have long to wait,' Skinner responded. Rafe turned to him. 'You're sure all the men are in place and know just what to do?' he said.

'Sure. I got all the strategic points covered. But as soon as anybody reaches the pass, they're gonna be blown way out of their saddles.' Rafe turned to him with an ugly leer.

'Just make sure nothin' goes wrong,' he muttered.

★ ★ ★

It was a relatively small party of riders that set out from the *Barbed S*, with Sheriff Snelgrove in charge — a number of men having been left behind to safeguard the ranch. The trail left by the self-styled Bronco Boys was clear to everyone, and they rode at a steady pace. From time to time Westoe looked at Stroup. He would have liked to know what the ranch-owner was thinking. It was an odd situation in which he found himself, going up against his own son.

Although he had made an effort not to give too much away, the pain he felt was obvious. His appeal to Rafe in the aftermath of the attack on the *Barbed S* was sufficient proof. Westoe was glad he wasn't in Stroup's shoes; he didn't know how he would have coped with the situation. What was perhaps even more to the point was what Stroup intended doing once they caught up with Rafe. Maybe he was too numb to have thought it through. While he was reflecting on these matters, Howe rode up alongside him.

'One way and another,' he said, 'it ain't gonna take too long till we reach wherever those coyotes are hidin' out. I hope Snelgrove knows what he's doin'.'

'I figure he ain't sheriff for nothin'.'

'I guess not.' He paused. 'What about you?' he continued.

'How do you mean; what about me?'

'I know you said you were just passin' through before you got mixed up in this mess. I was just kinda wonderin' if that was still the case.'

'I don't know,' Westoe replied, 'I ain't rightly thought about it. Hell, we'll be lucky to come out of this whole affair alive.' He suddenly grinned. 'Assumin' we do, there's somethin' else we have to do.'

'Yeah? What's that?'

'See about fixin' that cabin of yours.'

Howe laughed. 'I'll hold you to that,' he said. Westoe did not reply and they carried on in silence.

The trail got rockier as they rode up into the hills, and the sign they were following became harder to discern. There were other markings and from time to time Snelgrove called a halt and slid from his horse to take a closer look. Westoe's attention was no longer occupied in thinking about Stroup. As they got deeper into the hills, he was on the lookout for any indications of the outlaws' presence. The terrain was such that it wouldn't have been too hard for them to set an ambush, and Rafe would be foolish not to anticipate at least the possibility of being pursued. His keen eyes swept the hillsides, but he could see nothing untoward. At one point his attention was interrupted once again by the oldster.

'How many of those varmints do you reckon we'll have to deal with?' he said.

'There's no way of knowin', but there was a lot more of them than there were of us when they hit the *Barbed S* and there were probably others left behind.'

'I sure hope we ain't settin' ourselves up.'

'We've got a plan. Snelgrove's in charge. I guess he's got experience.'

They had discussed the matter before leaving the *Barbed S*. What they had come up with, such as it was, had been mainly down to Snelgrove. It had seemed reasonable enough in theory at the ranch house; it didn't seem quite the same in practice in the gathering gloom of the hostile hills. The afternoon light was fast fading when Snelgrove held up his hand to bring the posse to a halt.

'It'll soon be dark,' he said. 'The way

we figured it, night is the best time to strike at those varmints. We can't be too far off now. We'll carry on ridin' as long as we can see to follow the trail, then we'll make the rest of the way on foot.'

'They might have posted guards,' Barnet said. 'Maybe they already know we're here.'

'I don't think so,' Westoe replied. 'I've been keepin' a close lookout and I haven't seen anythin'.'

'There's no point in worryin' about it,' Snelgrove said. 'We'll just have to do like Westoe; be careful and keep our eyes open.'

They spurred their horses and moved on. The narrow valley they were riding through was filling with shadows and the walls seemed to pen them in with an oppressive weight. It was getting more and more difficult to see and follow the sign and they couldn't be entirely sure they were still on the right track, especially as the trail seemed to lead straight towards a solid wall of rock. Westoe wondered whether they hadn't entered a box canyon and would have to make their way back. Finally, as night's curtain was finally drawn across the landscape, Snelgrove decided the time had come to dismount. When they had done so, they hobbled the horses and then prepared to proceed on foot.

'No unnecessary talkin' from now on,' Snelgrove said. 'It ain't likely anyone will be watchin', but we don't want to take any chances.'

Taking their rifles, they moved forward.

The tracks made by Rafe and his gunnies had faded and it was hard to be sure they were still following their marks, especially in the dark. They seemed to be heading towards an impassable barrier which marked the far end of the narrow valley and Westoe wasn't the only one to think they must have gone wrong. They carried on a little further then Snelgrove stopped. He kneeled down, peering closely at the ground.

'Look here,' he whispered. The others

bent down to see. 'What do you think?' he asked.

'I ain't no expert in readin' sign,' Howe replied, 'but I'd say they were ridin' single-file at this point.'

'Yeah. And the way I see it, that means there must be a passage through that rock wall that only allows one rider through at a time. We just can't see it from here.'

There was silence for a few moments while the others considered the import of his words. It was Westoe who voiced their concerns.

'If that's the case,' he said, 'It would make an ideal place for an ambush.'

'They could be waitin' for us right now,' Drabble said. Barnet looked all around.

'Do you figure they could have seen us already?' he murmured.

'I don't reckon so,' Snelgrove replied. 'We did the right thing leavin' our horses behind and it's real dark. In any case, it doesn't matter because we ain't gonna fall into their trap.'

'So what do we do?' Bunch whispered. Snelgrove glanced up at the hillside. 'How are you boys for climbin',' he said.

'Looks pretty steep,' Barnet retorted.

'The only alternative is to go back, and I don't think any of us want to do that,' Westoe said. 'At least let's give it a try.' Snelgrove looked at the rest of them.

'We're with Westoe,' Sumter said. The sheriff nodded.

'OK,' he said, 'Then we're agreed. But remember not to make a sound. We're doin' too much talkin'. If we're right about this, Rafe's boys aren't far away.'

At the mention of Rafe's name Snelgrove glanced towards Stroup. Since commencing the ride he had hardly spoken. He was standing just a little apart from the others, his head slightly drooping. He had no time for further reflection, however, because Snelgrove, leading the way, had already begun the climb.

185

It was a difficult business, made all the harder by the darkness and the over-riding need to keep silence. At first they followed Snelgrove's route, but soon they spread out, each man seeking his own way up. They made progress in a crab-wise fashion, bent over on all fours and taking advantage of whatever hand and foot holds they could find. Although the ground was generally firm, it was still difficult at times to prevent their feet slipping from under them. At various stages one of them took a slide but was able to arrest his fall by clinging on to patches of brush or rocks. It was only when they began to approach the top that they were presented with a serious difficulty. What had not been obvious by looking up from the valley floor was an escarpment of seemingly sheer rock surmounting the hillside. Gathering their breath, they looked along it, but at no point did it seem to offer an easier way up.

'Let's follow it a little while and see if there's a way up,' Snelgrove whispered.

They began to scramble along the hillside and after following the line of the escarpment for a little way Snelgrove held up his hand.

'There might be a path here,' he said. 'Looks like there's been a rock fall sometime.'

'I figure it's as good a place as any,' Barnet remarked.

Without further ado Snelgrove began to pick his way among the fallen rocks and the others followed. At first the going was relatively easy, but as they climbed higher the rocks grew fewer in number and there were bald areas of earth and scree. They had to reach to find footholds and carrying their rifles became a real problem. Still they managed the ascent. At one point Westoe, poised awkwardly on a narrow projection, looked down into the dark depths of the valley below. He felt a sudden surge of vertigo and pressed himself hard against the cliff face. In a moment it had passed. Taking a deep breath, he reached out for the next hand-hold and levered himself up. He had lost track of where he was so it came as something of a surprise when he heard Snelgrove's voice coming from just overhead.

'Swing your leg over to the left. That's it. Now grab hold of that tree root and pull yourself up.'

Almost blindly he did as Snelgrove suggested and in another moment felt the sheriff's strong arm seize hold of him as he was hauled over the edge of the escarpment. He lay for a few moments, getting his breath back, and then raised himself to his feet. In addition to the sheriff, Bunch and Barnet had already made it to the top and with some assistance from them, the others scrambled up.

'I wouldn't want to do that too often,' Barnet muttered.

They took a few minutes to recover from their exertions before looking around. It was hard to distinguish details, but they had come out on the crest of a ridge. Fortunately, the ground on the other side descended at a much gentler angle to the floor of another valley which was shrouded in darkness. Somewhat to their surprise, Snelgrove produced a pair of field-glasses and clapped them to his eyes. After a few moments he put them down again.

'I think we're in luck,' he said.

'Can you see something?' Westoe asked.

'Here, take a look yourself.' At first Westoe could not make anything out, but when Snelgrove directed him he finally discerned the shadowy outlines of some buildings.

'I figure that must be the outlaw roost we're lookin' for,' the sheriff commented. 'I don't see what else they could be.' He passed the glasses around for the others to take a look. When they had done so he swept the surrounding hillsides.

'There's no way of bein' sure, but I think I can see what might be the entrance to the valley. If Rafe and his boys have set out guards, they'll be over in that direction.'

'What are we gonna do?' Bunch asked.

'What we came for,' Snelgrove replied. 'Bring those varmints to justice. This is the ideal time to creep up on 'em unawares. We should be safe from detection so far as any guards might be concerned, but remember to keep silence — especially when we get close to those buildings. Is everybody OK?' The others nodded in assent. 'Right,' he muttered. 'Let's go.'

With a final look about them, they commenced the descent. Although the hillside was quite steep, it was a lot easier going down than it had been coming up. The hill was dotted with vegetation and the lower slopes were clothed with trees. They were soon among them and the darkness became even denser while the sound of rustling leaves seemed to emphasis the menacing silence. They pushed onwards till the trees thinned and they had their first clear view of the buildings they had seen from the top of the hill. They consisted of a number of run-down shacks and cabins with a corral containing a number of horses.

'There aren't as many horses as I would have expected,' Snelgrove whispered.

'That's probably because some of the outlaws are waitin' at the pass to ambush us,' Westoe replied.

'Let's hope you're right.' Snelgrove didn't take much time weighing up the situation. He had a rough plan already formed and circumstances seemed to be playing into their hands.

'Here's what we do,' he said. 'Bunch, get over to the corral and get ready to turn the horses loose if I fire a shot. The rest of us will work our way around to the front of the cabins and take cover.' He glanced at Stroup. 'Remember, we're here in the cause of justice. I don't want any unnecessary bloodshed so I'm gonna challenge them to come out with their hands up. I'm hopin' that's what they'll do. If not and they start shootin', we'll respond but try to avoid causin' too many casualties. Is everybody happy with that?'

'Sounds OK to me,' Barnet responded for the rest of them. 'We'll still be outnumbered, but we have the element of surprise. With any luck, we'll catch 'em cold.'

'There's still the little matter of those guards up on the hillside,' Sumter said. 'If we have to start shootin', they'll soon be on their way.' Snelgrove smiled grimly.

'Then let's hope we don't have to do that,' he replied. He exchanged glances with the others. 'OK,' he said. 'Let's do it.'

They were about to move when Stroup unexpectedly spoke. 'Let me go on alone,' he murmured. The sheriff looked at him in some surprise.

'Why would you want to do that?' he said.

'Despite everythin' that's happened, Rafe is still my son. Maybe I can talk to him. Maybe I can get him to see sense and give himself up.'

'I don't see it,' Snelgrove replied. 'You'd only be puttin' yourself at risk.'

'And us too,' Drabble remarked. 'You seem to be forgettin' it was Rafe who led the attack on the *Barbed S*.'

'I don't care about the risk,' Stroup replied. 'I'm past all that. All I want to do is make one last appeal to him. Surely it's worth a try?'

'I don't like it. You'd be makin' yourself a sittin' target,' Snelgrove replied. 'We've got a plan. Let's stick to it.'

There was a moment's intense silence and then suddenly Stroup turned and began to run towards the nearest shack. Snelgrove tried to grab him as he went past, but the rancher was too quick. Snelgrove's reactions were instant.

'He'll have to take his chances. Now do as we said.'

Instantly they sprang into action, slipping away into the shadows and seeking for the best cover available.

Glancing back, Westoe could see that Stroup had ceased running and seemed to have come to a halt. After a few moments he began moving again, but this time his stride was slow and purposeful. It gave them a chance to get into position before Stroup appeared in the open before the nearest cabin. For a brief moment Westoe considered taking a stand beside him, but he quickly put it aside as quixotic. Whatever transpired, there was no room for gestures. He glanced across at where his companions had taken shelter and then raised his rifle.

Stroup continued walking and didn't halt till he was right in front of the cabin. The windows were dark and there was no way of knowing whether it was occupied or not. Westoe licked his lips. His throat felt dry and he was half expecting a blaze of fire to erupt from within the cabin. Instead the silence seemed to deepen and he almost started in fright when Stroup suddenly began to shout.

'Rafe!' he called. 'It's me, your father. I only want to speak to you. If you're in there watchin' me, then look; I'm throwin' away my rifle.' He raised the weapon and then hurled it from him.

'It's not too late,' he continued. 'Whatever you've done, whatever you've got youself into, it can be put right. You can still walk away from this. If it's the ranch you want, you can have it. It's yours. It doesn't matter to me.' He paused, as if seeking for the words that would finally get through to his son, but before he could do so he received his answer when flame suddenly appeared in an upstairs window and the shattering roar of a gun split the night. Westoe saw Stroup spin and fall to the ground. In almost the same moment a shot rang out in reply and instantly the whole place exploded in a fury of gunfire. The noise was deafening as lead whined through the air.

Westoe was firing rapidly while at the same time trying to aim his shots at the windows of the cabin. As far as he could make out, all the shooting was coming from the one cabin; the others remained shrouded in darkness. He could only assume that whoever had taken the shot at Stroup had thought he was alone. The question which worried him was whether that person had been Rafe. The rifle was hot in his hands as he paused to reload, and as he did so he heard fresh sounds and then the first horses came crashing round the sides of the building. He was momentarily surprised till he remembered it was Bunch's job to set them loose from the corral. Stabs of flame were continuing to issue from the windows of the cabin, but the rattle of gunfire seemed to have subsided. Smoke was billowing across the yard. He made another effort to see what had happened to Stroup, but it was impossible to make anything out clearly. He continued to concentrate his fire on the front of the cabin and was taken by surprise when the sounds of shooting began to resound from the rear of the cabin. It took him a moment to work out that it must be coming from Bunch, but it sounded like more than one gun was involved. How was Bunch doing back there? Then he guessed that the relaxation in the intensity of gunfire issuing from the cabin might be because the gunnies were attempting to make their getaway from the back. He glanced along the line to where stabs of flame indicated where Snelgrove and the others were carrying on the fusillade, and then began to slither away in order to get round the cabin and lend his support to Bunch.

Shots whistled overhead, but he was soon relatively clear and began to run, doubled over, parallel to the side wall of the cabin. He reached the back of the building and poked his head round the corner. Horses were milling about, providing him with cover. He stepped away from the shelter of the wall, conscious that he was putting himself in some danger not only from Rafe and his boys, but also from Bunch who might mistake him for one of them. As if to confirm his fears, as he made his way towards the corral two figures suddenly came into view and he swerved as their guns spat lead. Another shot rang out from nearby and, as one of the gunnies fell and as the other took to his heels, Bunch himself stepped out from the shelter of some bushes. He turned to Westoe.

'You're lucky I got good eyes,' he said. He took Westoe's arm and drew him into cover. 'Take a look,' he said. 'I think we've got them on the run.' Westoe peered through the bushes. He could see figures moving around in seeming confusion.

'They're lookin' for their horses,' Bunch said. 'I reckon they've been drinkin'. Snelgrove sure sized the situation up right.'

Even as he spoke a couple of them succeeded in springing aboard two loose horses and began to ride away. The space in front of the corral was emptying as the remaining gunslicks made their getaway, some of them, it seemed, on foot.

'Wait here,' Westoe said. 'Carry on shootin'.'

'Why, where are you goin'?'

'To check inside the cabin.'

He took a moment to survey the scene and then broke from cover. He quickly regained the angle of the building but, concentrating on what he was doing, he barely noticed a loose horse till it was almost upon him. Desperately, he tried to press himself against the wall of the cabin but he couldn't avoid a collision as the horse smashed into his side and the rifle was torn from his grasp. He fell to the ground, and in almost the same moment heard the boom of a rifle shot. The horse let out a loud whinny of pain as it took the bullet which had been meant for him but continued to plough on. As he struggled to raise himself to his knees, he saw the shadowy outline of a man with an upraised rifle bearing down on him. He struggled to support himself on his arm but it gave way beneath him and he fell to the ground again. He realised it must have been damaged in the collision with the horse and that for the moment he was helpless as the man with the rifle stood over him. He looked up over the barrel of the rifle that was pointed at his chest and felt a stir of recognition.

'You're Rafe Stroup,' he murmured. The man's face creased in a wolfish grin. 'Right here and now, that ain't any concern of yours,' he replied.

Westoe's only faint chance was to try and postpone the moment when Rafe's finger would close on the trigger, and he was desperately thinking of a reply when Rafe suddenly bent down and peered closely at him. His features changed and the wolfish grin became an angry snarl.

'I think I know who you are,' he rapped. 'You're the one that started all this.' He peered closely again. 'And if I'm not mistaken, you're the same one who showed up at the *Barbed S* lookin' for a job. Hell, I should have realised who it was right then.'

There was no time for Westoe to reply as the man suddenly swung his boot and brought it crashing into his midriff.

'Go on, admit it.' He lifted his leg and this time kicked him hard on the side of the head. Through waves of pain Westoe sought to maintain his senses as Rafe's features contorted once again.

'What happened to Oliver?' he suddenly rapped.

'Dwayne Oliver? If you'll give me a chance, I'll tell you.'

Rafe's response was to spit on Westoe's prostrate form and press the muzzle of the rifle against his chest. Westoe knew that there was nothing he could do and tried to brace himself against the killing shot that was about to come. Instead, he heard a voice which rang out from somewhere close by.

'Don't do it! I've got you covered.

Drop the rifle right now!' Rafe remained silent for a brief moment and then began to laugh.

'What are you gonna do, Pa? Shoot me?' he replied. He lifted the rifle and turned slowly round.

'Get away from that man!' Stroup replied. Rafe laughed once more.

'You're a fool, Pa,' he said. 'I don't know how you did it, but you should never have come here. That was a big mistake.'

Waves of darkness threatened to overwhelm Westoe as he struggled to try and do something, but he was helpless to affect the issue. Stroup's voice rang out once more.

'Why?' he said. 'Why did you have to do all this? I'm your father. You only had to ask and it was yours.' Rafe's laughter redoubled and Stroup seemed to let it run its course before he spoke again.

'One thing you must tell me. When you shot your brother, was it by accident or was it on purpose?' There was no response, not even another burst of laughter, and when Westoe raised his head it was to see the rifle pointed straight at his chest again.

'You ain't gonna stop me,' Rafe called. 'Nothin's gonna stop me now.'

Westoe closed his eyes as a rifle roared. For what might have been a moment or an eternity he thought he was dead, and then opened his eyes to see Rafe squirming on the ground. Blood was pouring from his thigh and he was screaming obscenities in a high-pitched voice. The Sharps rifle lay beside him but as he struggled to reach it a boot was clamped firmly across his arm.

'You made me do it,' Stroup almost sobbed. 'I didn't want to have to do it. You made me.' He bent down and picked up the rifle and then turned to Westoe. 'He made me do it,' he sobbed. 'I couldn't let him kill you in cold blood, could I?'

Westoe heard the sound of running footsteps and thought it must be some of Rafe's gunnies. Instead he heard the voice of Snelgrove.

'Is that you, Stroup? I thought you must be dead.'

'Westoe here is injured,' Stroup replied.

'Hell, ain't that Rafe?' another voice exclaimed.

There was no response and then Westoe felt himself being lifted by his arms and legs and carried away from the scene, whether into the cabin or into Leonae's trading store his jumbled brain found it hard to distinguish.

He didn't know for how long he had been unconscious, but when he came round a bandage was wrapped round his head and some kind of poultice applied to his midriff.

'I wouldn't try movin' too much,' a voice said. 'Your stomach is pretty badly bruised.' He looked up. The voice belonged to Howe and the other members of the posse were gathered behind him.

'Where am I?' he mumbled.

'Inside the cabin.'

He glanced round. The place was run-down and dirty, but surprisingly well furnished. Pale light was coming though the shattered window and he deduced it was early in the morning. Then he began to recall the night's events.

'What happened to Stroup?' he asked.

'Holden's OK. He got winged by a bullet, but there's no real harm done,' Snelgrove replied. He paused and looked at the others before continuing. 'Rafe's leg is shattered, but he'll pull through.' He stopped awkwardly and Barnet added:

'His father is in the next room with him now.'

Westoe was still feeling a little dizzy and Drabble came towards him with a mug in his hand containing strong black coffee.

'Take some of this,' he said. 'It might help.' Westoe raised the mug, but it didn't reach his lips. Before he could take a sip there was a sudden loud bang which seemed to shake the cabin to its foundations.

'What the hell . . . ' Snelgrove began. He got no further as the place was rocked by a second and a third explosion and then a series of massive booms. Westoe's head seemed to split open in response and a few of the others instinctively flung themselves to the floor. Outside, a series of flashes lit up the empty window frame. The deafening noise seemed to go on for an aeon, but finally it stopped and the ensuing silence seemed to hurt their ears almost as much. For a few moments nobody spoke as they regarded one another with startled expressions. Nobody could think of anything to say until Howe ended the hiatus.

'Well,' he said, 'I guess we were right about those varmints settin' up an ambush. I'd be willin' to bet they booby-trapped the pass.' Snelgrove and Drabble exchanged glances.

'I'd say you were right,' Snelgrove replied. 'They must have used the same dynamite they used to blow up the bank.'

'Looks like they got caught in their own trap,' Barnet said. 'I guess the ones that were assigned the job of guardin' the pass got confused when their own men began to appear.'

They lapsed into silence again, shocked by what had occurred, but gradually normality began to seep in with the gathering morning light, and with it a sense of relief. Nobody had been badly hurt in the previous night's shootout and it was obvious that there would be no more trouble from Rafe and his gang. All that remained was to take Rafe and those gunnies who had been rounded up and placed under arrest back to the County jail at Desolation Wells. Only the presence of Holden Stroup and their understanding of the pain he must be feeling kept their spirits in check. As they prepared for the ride back, Howe approached Westoe.

'Where to next?' he asked.

Westoe raised his head from his hands and managed a grin. 'Like I said before,' he said. 'We've got a lot of work ahead of us puttin' what's left of your ranch to rights.'

'You don't need to concern yourself about that,' the oldster replied. 'I reckon I'll manage.'

'Once we've done that, I figure you might need someone to help run the place,' Westoe added.

Howe looked at him. After a few seconds it was his turn to grin. 'You mean it?' he said. His eyes brightened. 'Hell, between us I reckon we could make a real going concern of it.' Westoe attempted to laugh but was brought up short by the sharp pain from his bruised stomach.

'One other thing,' he said.

'Yeah. What would that be?' Howe asked.

'Do you figure Leonae might be gettin' kinda tired of patchin' me up?'

The oldster's gap-toothed grin broadened as he replied.

'I figure she'd be more than willin' to give it another try.'

We do hope that you have enjoyed reading this large print book.

Did you know that all of our titles are available for purchase?

We publish a wide range of high quality large print books including:
Romances, Mysteries, Classics
General Fiction
Non Fiction and Westerns

Special interest titles available in large print are:
The Little Oxford Dictionary
Music Book, Song Book
Hymn Book, Service Book

Also available from us courtesy of Oxford University Press:
Young Readers' Dictionary
(large print edition)
Young Readers' Thesaurus
(large print edition)

For further information or a free brochure, please contact us at:
Ulverscroft Large Print Books Ltd.,
The Green, Bradgate Road, Anstey,
Leicester, LE7 7FU, England.
Tel: (00 44) **0116 236 4325**
Fax: (00 44) **0116 234 0205**